LIBREX —

Also by Elizabeth Hawkins

Sea of Peril
The Maze

ELIZABETH HAWKINS

RUNNER

 ORCHARD BOOKS

ORCHARD BOOKS
96 Leonard Street, London EC2A 4RH
Orchard Books Australia
14 Mars Road, Lane Cove, NSW 2066
First published in Great Britain in 1996
© Elizabeth Hawkins 1996
The right of Elizabeth Hawkins to be identified as the
author of this Work has been asserted by her in accordance
with the Copyright, Designs and Patents Act, 1988.
A CIP catalogue record for this book is available
from the British Library.
ISBN 1 86039 181 8 (hardback)
ISBN 1 86039 459 0 (paperback)
Printed in Great Britain

To Toby

Chapter One

"THIS IS THE third time I've called you, Nat. One of those fancy recordings, that's what I need: 'Nat – this is your mother, you are fifteen minutes and thirty seconds late, precisely.' Save my voice, it would. NAT! – *GET UP!*"

"Stop it, Mum."

Nat rolled over towards the wall and pulled the warm quilt up round his ears to block out his mother's voice. It still got through, like some high-pitched drone.

"The summer term – a new start you promised – no more getting late to school."

"I didn't promise anything," said Nat indignantly. He sat up in bed, blinking at the pale April sunshine struggling through his murky window.

His clock showed 8.45 a.m. The alarm had gone off; he must have heard it and gone back to sleep. He laughed.

"It's no laughing matter! I've had years of that

1

Miss Milburn on my back, complaining of your being late."

"She's gone, Mum, retired – we won't see any more of her."

"There's this new education officer, Mr Prendergast. A fresh start, I said, but look at you – second day of school and you're back to the old ways."

"Shut up, Mum."

"Don't you speak to me like that, son," Mum's voice was rising to a shriek. "I try hard enough. Ever since your father went, they've been watching us, seeing we're doing all right ... and you don't help." Her voice caught with a sob. "I'm worried about you, Nat. I want you to turn out good, be a good boy."

Nat wished Mum would leave off his father. It was bad enough having his father's dark suit hanging all these years in his room – because it was his wedding suit and cost a lot, and might fit Nat when he was older. A reminder of someone Nat had kicked out of his memory light years ago.

Nat caught Mum's eye, staring owl-like with its smudging of grey eye make-up. He scrambled into his school clothes and picked up his sports bag.

"What about something to eat?"

"Haven't got time."

"Yes, you have. There's a fried egg sandwich I cooked for you half an hour ago. I'm not having you eating sweets all day."

"You can go to work, Mum. I can get myself to school."

"I've heard that one before! And don't forget about Mr Prendergast, at the Social Services office after school. He's expecting you."

He'd forgotten! He'd arranged to meet his crowd after school on the allotment. Maybe he'd skip Mr Prendergast. Mum wouldn't know, or not for a while.

With the cold egg sandwich clamped between his teeth, Nat helped Mum slam the stiff front door.

"Got your key, Nat?"

"Yep."

"You won't let me down now, Nat, will you?"

The grey smudges round Mum's eyes were spreading into tired, shadowy circles.

"No, Mum."

He'd have to get Gemma in the break. She was usually the messenger, as the teachers never suspected her. They could meet a couple of hours later, after tea instead.

"You're a good boy, Nat."

He picked up his bag, and ambled after Mum's clattering high heels. Anyone could hear her a mile off on the concrete walkway outside the flats, since she'd had the steel tips put on her heels to save money in shoe repairs.

It was maths. Nat wanted to understand but he couldn't. Miss Barnes was walking between the rows of tables.

She stopped beside him.

3

"Nathan. Nice to see you in time for once! How are the equations going?"

"All right," Nat muttered, trying to curve his back to keep her eyes off his work.

He hadn't done much of it. He couldn't make head or tail of this stuff.

"Let me see, Nathan," Miss Barnes's gentle but firm hand pulled his shoulder back as she bent over his book. "There's not much here – and ... and it isn't right. You haven't understood it, Nathan."

Nat watched her slim finger pointing under the meaningless numbers. The pink of the nail was clear, unlike Mum's white-spotted and ridged nails, and the clean white rim was smooth and curved.

Miss Barnes straightened up and looked down at him, as if pondering some unfathomable mathematical problem.

"Nathan," she said quietly, "come and see me after school today and let's see if we can find a way of sorting this maths out. You've missed so much these last two terms, you can't handle this. It's like building a wall, maths, you can't put bricks on top without the ones underneath being there. Your underneath ones are missing."

Nat didn't say anything. He knew that.

Maths came after French and he couldn't stand French with Fish Face – the endless questions about how many "frères" and "soeurs" he had, and what his "père" did. If he skipped French, he went down to the market with Sean. It wasn't his fault if maths was timetabled after French most days.

He hadn't meant to get so behind with maths.

And in front of him sat Chas Mackenzie in his clean white shirt with iron-sharp creases down the arms, twice as thick as Nat, and he was getting it right.

"Good, Charles ... that's good work. Just a careless mistake here – what did you think ...?"

It was sickening. If Chas could do it, he knew he could do it, and better. But none of it meant a thing to him, these equations.

Nat opened his geometry set and pulled out his compass. He leant forward and carefully dug the spike in Chas's back. Chas leapt up screaming, a tiny spot of red on his white shirt, spreading and smudging.

Gemma was in the playground.

"You'll be in trouble now. They said if they caught you bullying again this term, you'd get suspension."

"Don't sound so pleased."

Nat was leaning against the goalpost. It shook behind him. He wasn't the tallest boy in the class, but he was the strongest. Strange, because Mum was small and thin and wispy. Nat had been born with a barrel chest, wide shoulders, strong thick legs, and feet so wide it gave Mum a headache trying to find trainers to fit. Perhaps his father had been built like him, but he'd never ask Mum. As far as he was concerned, the less he knew about him the better.

"My mum says she's sorry for your mum."

"Get off it. It was only a pinprick. Chas Mackenzie's a right crybaby."

"Well, it wasn't a great thing to do, was it? Chas wasn't bothering you."

Nat shrugged.

Gemma stood in front of him, arms akimbo, as she always did when she cornered him. She had been looked after by the same childminder as Nat had, been at the same nursery and primary and juniors, and still she was prepared to hang around with him.

"Gemma, tell the others to make it to the allotment later, after tea."

"We said after school."

"I've got to do something."

"Do it later."

"I can't. It won't wait."

Gemma tossed back her frizzy hair and frowned. Then the bell rang for the end of break and Nat started to move away.

"I don't know why we always have to do it your way."

"Oh, go on, Gemma. Do me a favour?"

"Say please."

"Please ..."

Gemma opened her eyes and mouth wide. "Kill me dead! Did I hear 'please' from Nathan Price?"

"Scram, Gemma. Don't forget to tell Sean and Adam."

Gemma put her fingers to her nose and wiggled them at him. He liked Gemma.

Chapter Two

NAT SLIPPED away quickly after school. He had his pride; he didn't like his class knowing where he was off to. He pulled the crumpled piece of paper from his jacket pocket and spread it out on top of a wall.

> Education Welfare Office,
> Social Services Department,
> 2 Milton Road,
> Rombridge

Dear Mrs Price,

   Please remind Nathan that I am looking forward to meeting him on Tuesday, April 24th at 4.00 p.m., after school.

Yours sincerely,

A. Prendergast
Education Welfare Officer

Lazy creep!

Whenever there were complaints about him, Miss Milburn, in her scratchy suits, used to come round to their place in the evening. Each time, she insisted on the telly being off, got out her glasses and her green folder and said: "Nathan, this is simply not good enough."

Nat knew where he was with Miss Milburn.

This Mr Prendergast wasn't in the same league; he couldn't even be bothered to come round to the flat. Instead, he summoned Nat to the Education Welfare Office.

The offices in Milton Road were in a new building next to the police station and the magistrates' court. It was like a brick box with square plate-glass windows and a little fountain choking at the front.

A fat man in a navy jacket unlocked the door.

"Yes?"

"Mr Prendergast wants to see me."

The man stared Nat up and down.

"I expect he does. Got an appointment?"

He seemed disappointed when Nat produced the crumpled letter from his pocket. He took his time reading it.

"Seems he's expecting you. Up the stairs, right along the corridor, second door on left – and no writing on the walls, no going where you're not wanted and no vandalism."

Nat found the room, but it was empty. He sat down in the swivel chair behind the desk. It suited him. He should rig up a chair and desk in the hut on the allotment. Head people had desks.

He pulled open a drawer. In it there were a cheese and tomato sandwich, a banana turning black, and an opened packet of Niblets. The files were scattered underneath. Definitely not up to Miss Milburn ...

The sun was blocked out of the window as a huge shadow fell across the desk.

"Do you like people going into *your* things?"

Nat almost jumped out of the chair. It was a deep, resonant voice. Slowly, he raised his eyes. The biggest man Nat had seen this side of the television screen towered over the desk.

Nat grunted.

"Sorry, I didn't hear you ..."

The voice echoed like thunder.

"Do you like people looking at your stuff, un-invited?"

"Dunno."

"Well, I *do* know and I *don't*."

A huge brown fist stretched down and slid the drawer shut.

"You must be Nathan Price. Let's sit on the chairs round the table in the window."

The man was a giant. The tie was loose on his collar, as if it couldn't contain the wide neck that burst up like a tree trunk. The neck was almost as wide as the stern face above it.

He had to be a heavyweight. Pity Grandad was dead – he knew all about boxing – but this Mr Prendergast had to be a heavyweight. Nat couldn't wait to boast to the gang.

9

Mr Prendergast's dark eyes bore down intently on Nat from across the table. His lips moved with animation, spilling out words: "... problems with non-attendance at school. If you miss out on school, Nathan, it affects your whole future. Who wants to give a decent job to a young man who can't write proper English, or who hasn't mastered essential mathematics? The choice is in your hands, not mine. Are you taking this in, Nathan?"

"Yep."

Of course Mr Prendergast must be an amateur – had to be – that's why he was doing this boring job, talking to idiots like himself.

The big man's voice rumbled on. He lowered his face so that his eyes were staring straight into Nat's, forcing him to listen.

Imagine meeting eyes like that across the ring! You wouldn't have a hope against a man like that: you'd have to resort to a few dirty tricks.

"Do you have any special interests or hobbies, Nathan?"

"Watching telly."

"And what do you like to watch?"

"Boxing."

"Do you now. I'm just a football fan myself. I can't bear to see people bashing each other's brains out." The man had to be joking! Nat allowed his mouth to lift in a smile, but Mr Prendergast didn't seem to notice. He was fingering a green file. "Before you leave, Nathan, there's a lot in your file here about some rather nasty bullying."

"It's lies."

"Perhaps you should read some of these reports yourself."

Sheet by sheet, Mr Prendergast went through the reports. He pulled out the one when Daniel Bridges's father had complained after Nat had given Daniel a going-over for laughing at his new haircut; and the one where whimpish Ella complained she'd starved all week when he kept shoving her out of the dinner queue.

There was nothing yet about Chas Mackenzie. When Mr Prendergast got to that one they'd be up to date.

"You've been suspended three times, I see. I don't believe this is the answer. I want you to work out why you let your anger get the better of you."

"Aren't I getting any more suspensions then?"

Nat didn't mind suspensions – they were like one long holiday from school.

"Any more of this bullying and we may send you to an excellent boarding school we know of in the country."

"You can't do that!"

"We can, Nathan."

The big brown eyes were watching Nat like the security cameras in the shopping mall. The smile had vanished.

"Mum ... she'll never manage without me."

Mr Prendergast looked taken aback. Then he stood up.

"It's in your hands, Nathan," he said, holding out his massive hand. Nathan's fist was lost in the enveloping grip. "Call me Ambrose," he smiled. "Are you usually called Nathan or Nat?"

"Nathan," said Nat suspiciously.

"Well, Nathan, I shall look forward to our meeting next month. Deep down I suspect you have a lot to offer."

Nat wheeled out of the office, down the stairs, past the fat doorman. Outside he pulled himself up on to the wall in front of the offices and extracted from his trouser pocket the packet of Niblets.

A shadow hovered at a window on the first floor. Nat held out the packet in front of him and finished the Niblets off. Then he screwed up the bag and threw it into the fountain.

Five minutes later a yellow Volkswagen tooted behind him. It was an ancient car with a rounded back. The huge shape of the driver filled it completely, tilting it so that the car almost touched the road.

The massive shape raised a hand and waved. Nat pretended he hadn't seen, but he saw quite clearly the sticker on the back window: *Jesus Saves!*

Nat was already halfway down Milton Road when he remembered.

Oh, no! He should have told Miss Barnes he couldn't come about the maths after school, but it had gone clean out of his head.

He leant on a parked car, head in his hands and kicked furiously, destructively, at the bulging front tyre.

12

Why couldn't he get anything right?

It was all a mess ... school ... home. It had been like that as long as he could remember. He was on the floor, and always would be, knocked down and out.

Chapter Three

NAT SAT through an agonising tea with Mum while she asked him question after question about Mr Prendergast.

"'Ambrose' – that's a funny name."

"He's a boxer – heavyweight."

"No, I don't think so, Nat. When would he get the time to train with a job like that? Ambrose ... The nuns at my school had a saint called Ambrose, I'm sure of it."

That fitted, with the *Jesus Saves!*

"There's no more marge, Mum. What am I going to put on my bread?"

His mother looked startled, like a cornered gerbil.

"Oh, Nat, I forgot it. No I didn't, I bought it ... I must have put it down in the post office. Sorry, love, can you make do with the strawberry jam?"

"That's finished too."

Nat stuffed a slice of bread in his pocket and pushed back his chair.

"Where are you off to?"

"Meeting Sean."

"You done your homework?"

"Sean and I, we're going to look at it together."

His mother pushed a strand of wispy hair from her forehead and frowned, but he knew he had won. He always did.

"Keep out of trouble then, and be back by eight-thirty."

Nat nodded as he yanked his jacket off the peg behind the door.

"And I mean that, Nat. It worries me terribly when you're not back when you should be. It'll be dark soon and the weatherman on telly says we'll have a freezing night . . ."

Her voice faded as Nat sprinted down the walkway.

After the bright sunny day, the air had turned cold. The moon and one star were already in the darkening sky. Nat loved to be out at this time. This was when the day was his.

He ran out of the estate, along Holmes Road and then climbed through the hole in the fence on to the allotments beside the railway line. His grandfather had told him that during the last war there had been a long queue of people hoping for an allotment to grow extra vegetables for their families. Now half the allotments had returned to wilderness. With so many parents working, it was quicker and easier to buy the vegetables in the supermarket.

15

The grass was newly sprouted, a limey green. One neat allotment had plants with fat little leaves bursting up through the freshly dug soil. A thin old man was bent double over the plants, tying string to sticks. He looked up and muttered to himself when he saw Nat.

"Now you keep off! These are my new broad beans, these are, planted last October and not to be ruined by some hooligan I knows," and he nodded sagely towards Nat.

"OK, Mr Birt," said Nat cheerfully.

He liked Mr Birt's allotment. Always digging and hoeing and raking Mr Birt was, an endless cycle of potatoes and beans, tomatoes and chrysanthemums.

"Mnn!" grunted Mr Birt, shifting the braces that held up his baggy trousers.

Nat took care to keep to the edge of the carefully tended plot.

Ouch! He ran straight into a fork. In the fading light he hadn't seen it standing erect at the end of a row.

"That's my fork," grumbled Mr Birt. "You put it back and watch where you're going. These is allotments, these is, not some kiddies' playground. Shouldn't be here . . ."

Nat could hear the noise from the hut on the abandoned allotment closest to the railway embankment. Gemma's shriek rose above Sean's giggle.

Nat dodged through the thicket of brambles that completely hid the old shed in summer and burst open the door.

"Well, here he is," said Gemma. "Superman! We were just about to pack it in."

"Where have you been then?" demanded Sean.

Adam sat in the corner glowering and watching. He wasn't a man for talk, Adam, but he was a rock in a fight.

"Called on the new education officer," said Nat casually, as he sat himself down on an upturned orange box. "He's a boxer – heavyweight."

"A boxer?" breathed Sean. He was older than Nat but small and skinny. He hadn't been long at their school. When he had arrived Nat had tried to show him what was what and demand his dinner money and take his sweets off him. That would have been enough for most kids, but Sean was like a tough little terrier, hanging on to Nat all the time, as if asking for more. After a bit it got to be a bore terrorising Sean, so Nat started taking him around with him instead.

"Yeah, a boxer. I reckon they thought I needed someone more my sort after Miss Milburn. But I'm still going to complain."

"Complain!" said Gemma. "But you're always complaining. That's nothing new. Have some Revolting Brew." She passed a mucky plastic bottle to Nat.

Gemma made up the Revolting Brew from cold sweet tea and fizzy lemonade or cola, and it was a truly revolting brown colour.

Nat took a gulp at the bottle.

"He's not doing his job properly, this Ambrose Prendergast."

Adam nodded his head in agreement.

"Course you've got to complain," said Sean.

"Hold on," said Gemma. "You can't complain if he hasn't done anything – what's he done?"

"It's what he hasn't done. First: he's too lazy to come to see me at home. Second: he says he's going to get rid of me at some prison school in the country. And third: he's admitted he's lazy. He said, 'You've got a lot to give.' Now I know my rights. I know what I should be getting out of this. He's paid to give *me* the attention, not *me* give *him* the attention."

"He did ask to see you ..." said Gemma thoughtfully.

"He doesn't know his job. It's because he's a boxer, so I might make allowances for that. He's got to find the time to train."

"What's he like then?" said Adam from the back of the shed.

"He's huge and dark and shiny like my gran's dinner table, and he's got fists the size of ..." Words failed Nat.

"Baking potatoes?" suggested Gemma.

"Like sledgehammers?" said Sean.

"Come on, this is stupid," announced Adam as he pushed past. "Nat kept us waiting hours and my old man is going to have it in for me if I'm late again. About time Nat thought of the rest of us waiting around ..."

"You sound like my mum," said Sean cheerfully. "But I'd better push off too."

18

"Sorry, Nat," said Gemma. "But if we meet this late, we're not going to have time to do anything."

One by one the gang trooped off, leaving Nat sitting in the deepening dusk.

They didn't usually do much in the hut, but it was their place where nobody bothered them. Nat didn't mind staying until it was dark.

The hut got darker and darker, while the night outside seemed light by contrast. A train rattled past, and from a distance came the muffled hum of traffic. A police or ambulance siren screamed into the night and faded away. Close by a car braked hard with a squeal of tyres.

Nat loved the noises of the night. Inside the shed it was quiet, except for the rhythm of his own breathing. The shed was his domain, his territory, where he could escape and dream. There was that night bird screeching again. He wished he knew what it was. The screech was closer, outside the door.

The door flashed back with a bang.

Nat started up, fists tight, expectant. In the doorway stood a gasping little figure, dark against the sky. It rushed at Nat with a stifled shriek. Nat was ready with a fist out, but the hot little body clasped his arm and clung to it, shaking and sobbing.

"Shut the door! Don't let them in! Say I'm not here!"

Moonlight filtered through the dirt on the window to show a small face surrounded by wet pale curls. Surely it wasn't raining?

Nat stretched out his hand. Not just wet curls, her

face was wet as well and she was panting. The little girl must have been running flat out. She was drenched in sweat.

"This is private," said Nat harshly. "No one's allowed in here."

"Please let me stay with you," the girl gasped between choking sobs. "They'll get me. You'll let me stay, won't you?"

Nat could make out the whites of her eyes, intense as lasers, boring into him, while her whole body shook with each pant.

"They're after me ... they'll get me. I'm too tired to go on and I'm lost and I said I'd help Mummy but they got her ..."

Nat moved towards the door. He'd soon see if someone was after her.

"Don't open the door!" she sobbed, her frightened voice dropping to a whisper.

Nat had his hand on the door when he saw a beam of yellow light travelling round the cracks of the door frame. He stood stock still and the light moved away. It reappeared travelling past the window, momentarily lighting up the orange boxes on the floor, and the magazines on the shelf. Nat and the little girl were too far into the corner to be touched by the beam.

He hadn't seen any faces, but he spoke softly.

"It's only Mr Birt, silly. He'll be checking up to see we've gone."

Mr Birt often called out something rude to them

when they made too much noise and it was time to go, but he didn't usually notice Nat staying on quietly on his own. If Mr Birt had invested in a torch, and was starting to get nosy, it would ruin Nat's evenings.

The girl slid to the floor with a sigh. Even Nat could tell she was exhausted. It was getting late and he had to get back.

"I'll take you back to my mum," he said with annoyance.

He hoped it would be too late for anyone to notice him walking with some bawling little girl.

"No!" the little girl yelped. "You don't see – they might be anywhere. I have to stay here. Please let me stay and I can go to sleep."

She had burrowed into the old cushions Gemma had rescued from a skip. She fished a small fluffy animal out of her trouser pocket and cuddled it against her tearful face. Her other arm she held tight around her chest. She started once, as if remembering where she was, looked up towards Nat so that in the faint light he saw the white teeth of her smile. Then her breathing deepened into a regular pattern and, even as Nat knelt beside her, she was asleep.

Nat stared at the glistening, damp little face.

Why hadn't he tried harder to kick her out? It wouldn't have taken much to do it; she was much smaller than him. A cold night, the weatherman had said. She was hot now but she would be freezing by the morning. Nat took off his jacket and tucked it in around her as best he could. He got up to go, but then,

21

on a second thought, placed the remaining Revolting Brew close beside her.

He'd have to get her out before the others came back again tomorrow. He'd never live it down otherwise.

Chapter Four

NAT SLEPT fitfully. The pale moon of a face, fringed with damp curls, drifted in and out of his consciousness. At the first buzz of the alarm he sat upright and remembered.

He had to get rid of that kid, get her out of the shed. Kids fiddled with stuff that wasn't theirs, and he wasn't going to have the gang's hoard of treasure played with by some little girl. She was a bother, a complication, something he could do without at the moment.

"Nat – you up already!" called his mum as she tried the bathroom handle. "You all right? You're not ill are you?"

Over breakfast she said: "I knew you'd get on with that Mr Prendergast. I'm glad you're starting the term well, Nat. It makes all the difference, getting off early in time for school. What's the hurry? You've got plenty of time to finish your toast."

Nat stuck the two halves of toast together, squashing the piece of fried bacon in the middle.

He pulled on his trainers, checked his football kit and made for the door.

"Let's walk together, love. You're so early I won't be in such a hurry. We can have a chat. You go out every evening and we never get a chance to talk."

"Can't, Mum. I've got – got extra French."

"Oh – I'm so pleased, Nat! That French teacher said you hadn't learnt a thing at the parents' evening. It's good to know a language. I never had the opportunity to learn one. With this European Market, they say every foreign word helps. Mr O'Riley, next door, he's worked in Germany and he says – Nat, wait! Have you got your dinner money?"

Nat waited impatiently while Mum searched for the term's dinner money that she had set aside in an old envelope.

"I'll take it tomorrow, Mum."

"No. I've got it ready. If I don't give it you now, I'll only be tempted to spend it at the supermarket. Here it is! Now, there's thirty-two pounds I owe in here. I know exactly how much is in here because I counted it last night, and every penny of it has got to arrive where it should ..."

Nat stuffed the envelope into his jeans' pocket and unlocked the door.

"Don't forget your key! What's that bacon sandwich for? Why don't you eat it here?"

Nat took the key off the peg by the door and slipped it into his jeans.

"Your key will fall out of there. Put it in the zip

pocket of your jacket. Where's your jacket? You haven't lost it! It cost me a fortune and I can't afford—"

"Bye, Mum," Nat said. "See you tonight."

"Bye, love," his mother sighed.

The girl was still asleep when Nat arrived at the shed. She looked so small and pathetic, curled up on the dusty cushions. Her hair was dry and lay in soft gold tangles. Her plump little child's face was smudged with dirt, and round her lips was the unmistakable brown moustache from the Revolting Brew.

Nat had expected to find her gone or at least awake, not peacefully sleeping, still wrapped in his big jacket.

He sat down beside her and listened to her gentle breathing. One hand still clutched the black fluffy animal, while the other lay outstretched on the dirt floor.

He picked up the hand and felt it. At least she was warm: the hand wasn't cold at all. It was a pudgy hand with soft fingers that disappeared in his grasp.

She turned her head and opened her eyes.

"It's you ... I knew you'd come back." She smiled at him with happy blue eyes. Then the smile vanished. She jerked up and gripped his hand. "They're not here? You haven't told them?"

"Listen," said Nat. He had to take a hold on himself and get rid of the kid. "I don't know why you're here, but you've got to go – back home."

"Why – why can't I stay?"

"You don't belong here, that's why. This is private property and we don't allow little kids in."

Tears sprang into the child's eyes and tumbled down her cheeks.

Tears didn't usually move Nat. He'd made enough children cry at school in his time. He felt in control when they got all upset, while he watched, coolly observant. But these tears worried him. He knew they weren't to do with him. Somehow that girl was hurting even before she'd set eyes on Nat.

"We'll find your mother."

"You can't," sobbed the girl. "They've taken her away."

Nat thought carefully and rubbed the little hand.

"The police have taken her away?"

"No – the men who were after her."

"We'll find your dad then."

"I haven't got one – he's dead."

Nat sat back. He hadn't got a father that he knew of, and even if he did still exist, Nat didn't want to know it. But he had Mum. This kid didn't seen to have anyone.

"What happened to your mum then?"

The child sat bolt upright and stared wide-eyed at him – and beyond him, as if remembering some awful dream. The small hand was clenched into a tight fist in Nat's palm.

"She was going to this big house, with important people. She was going to tell them about her discovery."

"What discovery?"

"A medicine discovery, silly. *Listen* to me! But these

bad men want her discovery and that's why they took her, I think."

Nat rubbed his forehead. It was all getting too complicated. He wished he'd got rid of her without asking anything.

"They're probably just some friends of hers."

"They're not. They're bad. Mummy says they want to steal her discovery, so that they can make her medicine and sell it to rich countries and get lots and lots of money."

"You know what I think," said Nat, a brilliantly simple idea dawning. "We'll go to the police. They can sort this out better than we can."

The little girl scrambled to her feet and made a dash for the door.

Just in time Nat blocked the doorway. Yet he wanted her to go didn't he? So why couldn't he let the dirty tear-stained little bundle out?

"What's wrong?"

"Let me go!" the little girl shouted, pummelling Nat's chest with her fists. "If you won't help me, let me go."

"But why not tell the police?"

"Mummy says the bad men have spies everywhere. They may be at the police station. I can't tell them."

"Are you sure you're not making this all up," said Nat coldly. It was beginning to sound like some film on telly.

"I saw them," gabbled the little girl. "Mummy sent me with the big envelope to the postbox, but the

27

gasmen were there digging up the road and I couldn't post the letter as the road was all shut off, so I went back and they were there with a big black car."

"Yes?" said Nat.

"I hid behind the hedge, but I saw through the branches and they pulled Mummy out of the house and a man had his hand over Mummy's mouth and she was crying ..."

"Go on," said Nat softly.

"And I called out to her, and they saw me, and – and they came after me so I ran and ran ..."

"And what do you think you're going to do now?" said Nat suspiciously.

"I'm going to wait until they've gone away and then I'm going ... to Salisbury,"

"Salisbury?" sneered Nat. "And what's in Salisbury?"

The girl stood with her head on one side, watching Nat carefully. "I'm going ..." Her face stilled as a thought came into her head. "I'm going," she said quickly, "I'm going to stay with my aunty. She'll look after me."

"And how are you going to get there?" said Nat laughing.

"I'm going on the train. I can hear the trains from here. And you can buy me a ticket. Is that sandwich for me – I'm very hungry?"

He'd already missed assembly, Nat realised when he saw the hand of the station clock move to 9.15. Why

28

on earth was he doing this? He must be crazy, allowing himself to be ordered around by some little girl who barged, uninvited, into his shed.

But there was something about her. She seemed trapped, with all the world against her. He knew how that felt. And he liked her tough brand of courage, those plump little fists hammering furiously on his chest.

But most of all, even though he didn't want to, he believed her.

There was something desperate about her that made him afraid that if he tried to take her to her mother or the police, he might never make it. She would run off as she had before, and heaven knows what hands she'd fall into. Yes – it was better for her to get to her aunty.

The queue to the ticket office wound forward, men and women in office suits, briefcases to hand, newspapers and umbrellas tucked under arms, shuffling towards the ticket office.

"Ticket to Salisbury," Nat muttered through the hole at the lady sitting behind the ticket desk.

"Single or return?"

"Single – child fare."

The woman looked up and pursed her red lips: "Eight pounds fifty. Shouldn't you be at school?"

Nat poked around in his dinner-money envelope and pulled out a ten-pound note. The lady took the note with a disapproving sniff and shot the ticket back through the slot.

Nat was panting when he got back to the shed.

He threw the ticket down at the girl. "I'm not doing that again, so don't lose it. Follow the track beside the allotments and you come to the station. I've got a timetable – you've missed the morning train to Exeter, that's the one that stops at Salisbury." Nat unfolded the timetable he'd picked up. "There's another in three hours' time, at one-ten."

"I haven't got a watch," said the little girl, her face quivering.

"Well, you're not having mine."

"I can't tell the time properly yet, unless it's on the o'clock."

Nat had to get away before she demanded anything else. What was it they learnt in cubs, about the sun's movements?

"Wait till the sun is directly above the hut," said Nat desperately. "That's the middle of the day. When the sun's overhead, set off for the station."

The little girl stood still and considered. The piercing blue eyes clouded over and then cleared with a dazzling smile. Nat wanted to be rid of her, but he was entranced as her face changed from utter misery to beatific happiness.

"I know," she cried. "You can come with me."

"Oh no!" said Nat. "Not on your life! I've done too much already. You're on your own. You've already made me miss first lesson at school and I'm in a lot of trouble from that already. You came pushing into this shed unasked, making a nuisance of yourself. I've done enough!"

He glanced at the trusting face gazing up at him. Shadows of hurt and fear flitted across it, as the little girl stared in bewilderment. Nat slammed the door and ran.

"Look where you're going," shouted old Mr Birt, spreading muck over his patch. "That's my broad beans your lot trampled last night."

"Can't be us. We're always careful."

And they were. Nat loved watching the plants grow on Mr Birt's neat allotment, so they always went round the edge.

"Well somebody did it, and you lot were here last night. Why aren't you at school, you blighter? In my day you'd have got the cane. They've gone soft these –"

No – he'd had enough of the girl, Nat decided. What he needed to do was get to school in time for maths.

Chapter Five

"I STAYED for an extra hour after school yesterday, Nathan, waiting for you to come."

Miss Barnes went on marking the exercise book on the desk in front of her. Nat gazed down at her neatly parted hair as the pen scribbled over the book he had just handed in.

"I had to go and see someone."

"Wasn't that someone meant to be me, Nathan?"

"No, it was someone else important." He was making a mess of this. "I wanted to come, Miss Barnes, but I forgot."

Miss Barnes closed the exercise book and looked up at him with a calm, grey-eyed stare.

"You forgot – and you forgot the time the class began this morning," she spoke slowly, carving out each word with precision. "Nathan, I don't *have* to stay after school to help children who are having difficulty with their maths, and even if I *choose* to give up my free time in this way, there are a number of children who would benefit from some individual tuition. Tell me – why should I bother with you?"

Nat wondered why himself. Miss Barnes was right: he was pretty well a lost cause. He said nothing and stared back at her.

"What do you suggest we do, Nathan?" Miss Barnes's voice had lost its edge. She looked directly at him.

"I can come after school today, miss. That's if you want me to."

"Let's try again, Nathan, shall we? After school then, at four-fifteen."

"We can't meet at the shed after school," Nat explained to Gemma in the lunch break. "I'm booked up this evening."

"Booked up again, are we?" said Gemma. "What makes you think we can't meet without you?"

"It's no fun without Nat," said Sean. "Are you sure you can't make it? I've got this new magazine my dad picked up."

They had a stash of computer magazines in their store at the hut. What they really wanted was to get their hands on a second-hand computer. They'd already drawn up a list of games they planned to try.

"Adam, you're coming, aren't you?" said Gemma.

Nat knew she was only trying to make a point, as the enthusiasm had drained from her voice.

"Nah," grunted Adam.

"Right then, we'll meet tomorrow," said Nat.

33

Nothing in the day was going as Nat had intended, so it didn't surprise him when a beige figure invaded the football game during PE.

"Right, stop the game!" yelled an irritated Mr Bingham. He blew a shrill blast on his whistle.

The headmistress's secretary extricated one high-heeled beige shoe from the muddy pitch.

"Is Nathan Price here?" she demanded.

"Nathan," bellowed Mr Bingham. "Where's Nathan?"

Nat sauntered forward. He guessed it was about Chas Mackenzie. He knew they'd catch up with him eventually. They always did. Surely they couldn't send him off to boarding school for a pinprick like that?

"You're to go home at once," said the secretary straightening her beige cardigan. "It's very urgent."

"Home?" exclaimed Nat, surprised.

"You're wanted at home, and the headmistress said you're to go at once."

"Is it Mum?"

"I don't know what it's about, but you're not to wait until the end of school."

Cold shivers ran up and down Nat's spine. It was his worst nightmare that something would happen to Mum. He gave her a hard time, but he did care; he worried about her looking so tired, about her having so little money. He knew she gave most of the food to him. He wanted to tell her he cared; somehow the time never seemed right, or the words sounded too silly.

34

He ran with his bag bouncing on his back all the way home.

There was a police car parked by their block. He looked up at the walkway outside the flat and he could see the door open. Mum must be back from work early or someone had broken in. As he ran up the walkway he noticed, parked behind the police car, an old yellow Volkswagen.

What on earth ...? Mr Prendergast as well? So it must be about him.

Breathless, he burst into the living room. It was like a scene from a photograph. Every face was frozen, staring in his direction. There was Mum and she had been crying. Mr Prendergast loomed massive, leaving little room for the two policemen beside him. A policewoman sat on the settee holding Mum's hand.

Then Mum set up a wail: "Tell them you didn't do it, Nat? It's a mistake ... You don't know her, do you?"

Mr Prendergast stepped forward and held his hand up to silence Mum. He exchanged a glance with one of the policemen.

"Nathan" – his booming voice was lower and quieter than Nat had heard before – "we have an extremely serious situation on our hands. Very serious indeed."

Nat stared up at him and at the hard faces of the policemen, shut tight against him. He'd been afraid it would come to this – it was what he'd always expected.

"I want you to listen carefully to PC Titchfield here, and consider before you answer."

The police officer cleared his throat and looked down at his notes.

"At eleven-fifty a.m. today," he read, "Mr Ray Birt was working on his allotment when he heard a cry followed by a short scream. The cry came from an abandoned shed on a neighbouring allotment. He thought it was Nathan Price and his friends, who meet regularly in the shed both during and after school hours. At one-thirty p.m., on returning from the garden centre with new broad bean plants to replace those trodden into the ground by Nathan and his friends the previous night, he heard groaning coming from the shed. As it continued unabated, he took it upon himself to investigate. He found a girl in the shed, aged approximately six years. She was unconscious from a wound on her head. She had been gagged with—"

The second policeman held up a plastic bag and gingerly removed Nat's jacket. Nat could see the dark stains spattered on the green sleeve.

"Is this your jacket, Nathan?"

Nat looked at his mother, but she avoided his glance and stared rigidly at the jacket.

"Yeah," Nat whispered.

"I didn't hear, Nathan. Speak up. We need to be absolutely clear." The first policeman laid down his papers and took a step towards Nat.

The room was silent, except for the yells of little

children playing in the yard below. The second policeman stood poised with a pen and pad.

"Yes, it is!" Nat yelled. What did it matter – they were going to trap him anyway.

"Now, Nathan, your mother tells us you were out early this morning, unusual for you, but the school register reports that you were several hours late for school. Is that correct?"

"Yeah."

"Mr Birt tells us he saw you at the shed, at the time you should have been going to school, and that you were carrying some bread in your hand, a sandwich I believe."

Nat didn't answer. He felt a cold glass shell fall into place around him, cutting him off from the rest of the world.

There was more rustling of plastic bags and the second policeman produced the half-eaten bacon sandwich.

"The girl was lying on this sandwich," said the first policeman taking the sandwich and sniffing it. "Bacon if I smell correctly."

Mum started crying in hoarse, rasping sobs. The policeman turned to her.

"Mrs Price, do you know anything about this sandwich?"

Mum looked up at Nat, as if pleading with him, but Nat, shut off behind the glass wall, ignored her.

"I told you ... Nat took it with him, to eat on the

way. I don't know what's gone wrong, I really don't. He's not how you think, he's a good boy ..."

The policewoman put her hand on Mum's arm and handed her a box of tissues.

"It's my sandwich and I gave it to her," Nat said coldly.

Why hadn't he stayed? She'd begged him to help. He'd only wanted to get to maths, to get out of trouble with Miss Barnes.

"So who is she, this girl?" said the policeman quietly, moving closer to Nat.

"Ask her."

"We can't. She's in a coma."

"Coma. Is – is she going to die?"

"It's a severe case of concussion. We don't know, Nathan. The next few days will be crucial."

Nat felt himself sway. He grabbed the table edge. The pale face with the damp matted curls, the blue eyes passing so swiftly from fear to shining happiness ... She had trusted him, believed in him. Chased and trapped.

He should have stayed and helped her. He should have gone with her to Salisbury.

Someone shook his arm.

"Nathan," said a deep voice above him. "Your mother and I have been talking. We think you'd be much better off at our school in the country."

Nat stared at Mr Prendergast's massive chest, at the tie heaving as he spoke.

"She has agreed with me that you're getting too much for her to handle. She loves you, Nathan, that's why she knows it's for the best if we take you into our care. You'll find there's a lot going on at our school, and you can stay there while the police investigate this dreadful attack."

"You're taking me away from Mum?"

"You can have tonight with your mum, to get some things together. I'll fetch you in the morning."

"You can't make me go," said Nat furiously.

"We can," said Mr Prendergast quietly. "In the morning we'll have a court order. This is a very serious charge, Nathan, and I've just heard of an attack you made yesterday, quite unprovoked, on a boy in your class. It's for your own safety—"

"Safety?"

"To protect you from yourself."

There was talking and discussion. Nat slumped in front of the TV in the corner, until the police left and only Mum and Mr Prendergast remained.

Suddenly Nat was furious. He leapt up and kicked the TV.

"You think I did it, don't you?" he yelled, his voice hammering through his head. "But I didn't! You never asked me."

Mum looked terrified.

"Your mother identified the rope the girl was tied up with," said Mr Prendergast calmly as he stood up and put on his jacket. "She says it was her old washing line from the balcony, which she had given you for the shed."

So someone had been into their treasure cupboard after all. Tied her up. She must have been terrified. Nat couldn't bear to imagine the tear-soaked little face. He stood still, paralysed by the picture.

And he had left her.

The door shut behind Mr Prendergast. Mum and he were alone.

"Mum?" She had scuttled into the kitchen. "You don't believe I touched that girl, do you?"

Mum glanced up with an agonised face and wept.

Chapter Six

"GOODNIGHT, Nat." His mother's muffled voice drifted through the locked door.

He needn't have bothered to lock it. Mum hadn't come near him all evening. She had a sitcom on the telly but he could still hear her sobbing against the fake telly laughter.

Was she waiting for him to go and explain that it was all a misunderstanding, that he hadn't done it? He'd noticed the hesitation in her: she didn't want to think he'd hurt the girl, but she wasn't sure any longer. What if he told her the truth and she didn't believe him? That would be the worst.

No – he had things to think about, without her.

He had always known it would come to this – he couldn't win. The girl was a muddle, but then so was everything else in his life. In some ways it made sense to give in and be counted out. There were some people who were never on their feet at the last round, and he was one of them.

The police in their navy blue, Mr Prendergast in his grey: the men in suits, they always had it their way. And he hated them.

Then he thought of the little girl, alone in an anonymous hospital bed. She wouldn't be able to tell them what she knew, and ... she might not recover. Someone had been out to get her.

Nat flushed with anger as he remembered her frightened blue eyes, and then the smile that flashed across her face so quickly when she was happy.

That little girl had been in his care. Whoever had hit the little girl, had demolished his life too.

He knew now he couldn't wait for the count and go off docilely tomorrow with Mr Prendergast. The girl had done nothing and he had done nothing. If only he could find out who was after her, he could surely prove he'd had nothing to do with it.

He could stay at home with Mum, go to Miss Barnes and catch up on maths – oh no! – Miss Barnes would have missed him again today.

That clinched it! He wasn't knocked down yet. He had to show them all that they were wrong, that he was in with the fight. He had to give himself one more chance.

Nat waited until Mum had stopped tossing and turning in her bed next door and the last footsteps of the pubgoers returning home had stumbled by outside. Gingerly, he unlocked his door and turned the handle.

The door squeaked as it swung open, he had meant to oil it ages ago. He tiptoed across to the airing cupboard, and pulled the doors back. The torch was there, on top of the electricity meter, where Mum could check how much electricity they were using.

The front door was unlocked: Mum had forgotten to lock it again.

As Nat sprinted down the walkway, a dog barked. It was a bright clear night again, with a cutting cold. Nat shivered without his jacket. There was no one much about, apart from a man walking his dog, stopping it at every lamppost where it refused to do its business. A couple of men in office suits swayed outside the pub on the corner. The pub had closed and they staggered past Nat, clinging to each other, singing. One grinned at Nat with a drunken wink.

The allotments basked in a silvery light, drained of colour. Nat edged round them. He didn't want to leave footprints on Mr Birt's freshly turned soil.

A train hooted in the distance, then rushed past on the embankment, a goods train with wagon after wagon rattling by. Nat sprang into its shadow, over to the shed.

His way was blocked. Someone had tied black and white striped ribbon to metal sticks set up around the shed. Nat lifted the ribbon over his head as he ducked underneath. The shed door was sealed too, with striped sticky tape. Nat found the top of the tape and peeled it down, laying it carefully on the ground.

He shut the door behind him, blocked the window

with cushions that were wet and sticky, and switched on his torch.

He had blood on his hands. It hadn't dried properly on the cushions; there must have been so much of it. Nat stared in horror.

Blood on his hands ... and they thought he had done this.

Then he saw the blood on Chas Mackenzie's shirt. No – it wasn't the same at all. Surely it wasn't the same.

The shed was in a terrible mess. The vegetable crates they used as seats had been chucked to one corner. Their treasure shelf with the computer magazines, their penknives, biscuit tin, code book, collection of rocks, had been pulled away from the wall.

Someone had been in there, throwing everything around.

The police couldn't have done it; they would never make such a mess of the place.

Nat crouched down and imagined he was the height of the little girl. What would she have seen? For a start, she would never have reached their shelf.

He shone his torch across the cracked wooden walls.

Gemma had decorated the walls with old posters, thrown out by the video rental shop. They stopped the draughts coming in. They were still in place over the cracks, even the one beneath the window which stopped up the gnawed mousehole. It was of E.T. Had the monstrous little spaceman frightened the girl? His fat tummy was bulging outward with the draught ...

In a flash Nat ran his hands across E.T.'s stomach. There was something in there!

He tore the poster down, and a big rectangular envelope dropped to the floor. Nat snatched it up and shone his torch on the front.

Professor Alan Keeping,
c/o Intervarsity Congress of Immune Deficiency,
Coghill Hall,
Lower Ebbsbourne,
Near Salisbury,
Wiltshire

FIRST CLASS MAIL: To await arrival.

Some aunty in Salisbury!

Nat was elated. He'd been right to come. It was the big envelope the gasmen had stopped the little girl from posting. She must have had it hidden on her. Then he remembered the plump outstretched hand and the other arm clasped tightly round her stomach. She'd had it under her sweater!

It was a sign for him, an omen, finding that envelope. It was the first thing he had got right in weeks.

No one was going to stop him now, neither Mum, nor Mr Prendergast, nor the police.

He would get whoever had hurt the girl, and he wouldn't only tell everyone they were wrong, he would *show* them, *prove* it and they would believe him.

He stuck the envelope under his shirt, slipped out of the shed and sealed up the door again with the tape.

Nat sat on his bed and prised open the envelope flap with his penknife. There were fifteen numbered, type-written sheets and they looked pretty boring, full of long words that meant nothing, medical, scientific stuff by the look of it. On the second page was a complicated chart, bristling with numbers and letters. Maths – he'd never understand that.

Attached to the front was a sheet:

Paper to be given by Dr Anne Buxton,
International Intervarsity Congress of Immune
Deficiency Disease, April 28–29.

CONFIDENTIAL: Not to be released prior to Congress.

Nat flipped through the pages. The only other names he could see were a long list of authors of books on the last sheet, under the heading of BIBLIOGRAPHY.

It was obvious: this Dr Buxton must be the girl's mother, and if she had been abducted, as the little girl claimed, that only left this Professor Keeping. He might know who else was interested in the envelope, and had been after this little girl.

Nat looked at his watch for the date – 25 April – and it was Wednesday. Twenty-five, twenty-six, twenty-seven, Nat counted on his fingers, the twenty-eighth was Saturday and the twenty-ninth was Sunday. This congress business had to be over next weekend.

He had two days, or at the most three, to find Professor Keeping.

That shouldn't be too much of a problem: Salisbury was on their rail line.

Nat chucked his football kit out of his bag, and stuffed in a sleeping bag still tightly rolled in its cover. Mum had bought it in the sales cheap for him to use camping with the Scouts, but he'd never made it to Scouts – the cubmaster had refused to recommend him.

He shoved in a T-shirt, a pair of pants, a big wool sweater Mum had found in the Oxfam shop, which he'd never worn because it was too hot and scratchy, and the torch. He counted his dinner money. He had just over twenty pounds left – more than enough.

He tiptoed across the bathroom and emptied the make-up out of Mum's sponge bag. He stuffed in his wet flannel, his toothbrush and the toothpaste tube on the side. Then he pulled the handle on the lavatory, just in case Mum wondered what he was up to.

Back in his room he examined the timetable he had picked up at the station that morning. It seemed light years ago now, another century.

The first train to Salisbury was at 6.45 a.m. It stopped everywhere, but he couldn't risk waiting for the 8.15 express. He needed to slip away before anyone noticed he was missing.

He set the alarm for six, kicked off his trainers, and climbed fully clothed into bed.

Chapter Seven

THE ALARM went at six. Nat hammered it before Mum could wake.

He'd slept badly again, listening out for the alarm, and he felt drained and tired. He struggled out from beneath his quilt.

Was he mad? They might at least have warm beds at this boarding school in the country . . . But no, as he caught sight of his kit bag standing ready and packed, he knew that he would not have the chance again.

He lifted the corner of the curtain. A weak sun was coming up but the street was deserted apart from a prowling dog. A woman cycled by, off early to work; and two men carrying briefcases ambled out of the estate and went to examine the timetable attached to the bus stop. They didn't look the sort who took buses: car owners more likely, probably from Social Security, checking on benefit claimants, keeping an eye on the people leaving for work. Nat had seen their type before around the estate.

Nat pulled on his trainers, strapped on the sports watch he'd found in the changing room at the school pool, and swung the kit bag over his shoulder. He couldn't risk banging the stiff front door, so he left it on the latch.

The curtains covering most of the windows in the block were still drawn. Nat walked purposefully across the yard, trying to look as if it was nothing unusual for him to be up at this hour. Keeping well back, he peered round the corner into the street.

A bus rumbled up, stopped at the bus stop and roared away.

The men were still looking at the timetable. Why hadn't they got on the bus?

One of them turned and stared up at the windows of Nat's flat. His companion leant towards him and said something in his ear.

The sun was shining straight into the face of the staring man and he shielded his eyes with a hand. As he turned back to the man beside him, he let his hand fall. He seemed to wink at Nat.

The drunks! The drunks from last night.

With their briefcases, white shirts and ties they looked unexpectedly fresh, with no hint of a hangover. The man couldn't have seen Nat, so how come he had seemed to wink at him?

But Nat was certain: they were waiting for him.

They must have been watching the allotments last night, seen him go into the shed, and shadowed him home. Of course! They must have found the girl in the morning after he'd left and, as she didn't have the envelope, thought she'd given it to someone else . . .

"Ooh, you gave me a fright!"

It was Craig Bentle.

"What you doing out this early, Nat? Your mum kicked you out?"

Craig would give him away!

Nat seized the boy, pinioned him against the passage wall, and covered Craig's thin mouth with his hand.

"If you make a sound, you're dead."

Craig bit Nat's hand.

"Get off, Nat!" he said as he wriggled free. "What's up? Here I am, walking peaceful like, round with my bag . . ."

Nat kept a tight grip on Craig's skinny shoulders. Craig was no pushover, he could wriggle his way out of anything.

"Craig . . . How'd you like a fiver?"

"A fiver?" Craig's pale eyes lit up. "Have you been nickin' things again?" He eyed Nat suspiciously. "What for?"

"Give me your bag. I'll do the papers down the street, past the bus stop, to that phone box round the corner."

"You want to deliver my papers?" said Craig in disbelief. "What have I gotta do?"

"You take my kit bag and drop it in the phone box, then stay away till I've finished. I'll pick up my bag and leave the newsagent's one in its place."

50

Craig scratched a protruding ear.

"What about the fiver?"

"I'll leave it in the bag."

Craig giggled. "You know something, Nat, you're loony. I'm not sure I trust—"

Nat pushed Craig back against the wall again. "You'll do it, or there'll be trouble today in school."

"OK ... OK, but don't forget my fiver."

"And I want your cap!"

Craig picked up the kit bag and strolled down the street. Nat watched one of the men stare at Craig and then shake his head at his companion.

Nat swung the heavy newspaper bag over his shoulder, pulled the peak of the yellow *Daily Mail* cap down over his eyes, and stepped out into the street.

Keeping his head down, he pulled out the first paper. It had a number two on it, which matched the first of the row of old houses beyond the flats. He tried to force number two into the letterbox, but it took an age to roll up tight enough and squash through. On the other side of the door a dog yapped and snarled.

The headband of the cap dug into his forehead. The cap was too tight and wet with sweat. It was going to take him for ever to stuff the papers through. He'd have to find a quicker way.

Nat took the next paper, for number four, and threw it on to the doorstep. He was approaching the bus stop.

Careful ... don't rush it ... look casual.

Nat was sure the men could hear his thumping heart

51

as he turned his back to them, pretending to look in his bag. He could feel them, still and alert behind him.

Another bus approached, braked.

"Hurry along, guv. Are you getting on or not?" called an impatient conductor to the men.

"No, we're not."

"It's only the number nineteen stops here, guv."

"We are expecting someone."

"Waiting are you? You should keep clear of the stop then. Wastes our time ..."

Ding! Ding! The bus roared off with a puff of black fumes – and the men were still there, behind Nat.

By the sixth delivery Nat was tempted to chuck the bag, together with the remaining papers, on the doorstep and run for it. He would have done that yesterday, but ...

Last chance, he reminded himself, your last chance. Be careful. No more risks. It was an effort being so careful, but he mustn't attract attention.

The kit bag was waiting in the kiosk. Nat was overjoyed. It was going all right. If Craig had been there he could have kissed him, like a footballer after a goal!

The fiver – he might need it. It was still a long way to go to Salisbury. But if he didn't leave the money, Craig might chase after him shouting or something.

Nat fumbled in the dinner-money envelope and found a five-pound note. He stuffed it into the newsagent's bag, but he kept the cap.

*

"Child single to Salisbury."

Nat shoved a ten-pound note, through the hole in the ticket office window.

The nosy woman of yesterday had given up her place to a man who sniffed and coughed and who sat there sucking a sweet and looking sorry for himself. He passed the ticket and the change back through the hole without a second glance.

Nat wandered down to the end of the platform. The station clock said 6.35 a.m. – ten minutes to wait.

A dazed woman with a suitcase stared up the track. A man in overalls leant against the station wall, peering at the newspaper he had folded back in his hand. Nat could make out part of the headline on the folded sheet:

CALLOUS ALLOT ...

Nat had to read it, had to know.

A door opened in front of him and a woman in an orange blouse, panting with effort, carried out a news-paper board. The letters were in bold black:

Bring back the cane!
CALLOUS ALLOTMENT ATTACK ON GIRL

The woman went back through the door and the lights inside were turned on. Through the window Nat saw the cafeteria, with magazines and newspapers displayed along the far wall.

He turned the door handle.

"Sorry, we're not open until seven," called the woman over her shoulder as she stacked biscuits on the counter.

"Just a paper—" began Nat.

"You heard me. Seven, I said," the woman pointed to the clock above the counter. "Twenty to seven," she said triumphantly.

"I've got the money."

"Are you trying to be cheeky, or something? The regulations say seven, and seven it is."

She turned a heavy face, chin wobbling, to look at Nat.

Nat bolted.

Why hadn't he thought to take a paper from Craig's bag? Could there be a description of himself?

He pulled the cap lower over his face and slunk down the platform to a bench at the far end. The station was filling up. He sat hunched with his shoulders up round his ears; he couldn't risk being recognised by anyone on the platform.

Nat jumped at a loud crackle behind his ear.

"The train approaching platform one, is the six forty-five from Waterloo," boomed the crackling voice, "stopping at Basingstoke, Whitchurch, Andover, Grateley, Salisbury, Gillingham, Yeovil and Exeter. All change at Basingstoke for Reading and Bath."

It seemed an age before the hoot of the train echoed in the distance and the nose of the engine appeared round the corner. As the train slowed to a stop, Nat grabbed the door of the carriage opposite him and leapt

54

up the steps. He sank with a sigh into a plush seat with a white cloth over its back.

Opposite Nat a pair of polished black shoes poked out from beneath a dark striped leg. Nat followed the leg up to a newspaper held out by two white hands framed by white cuffs with gold cufflinks. The train started up and gathered speed. The pale hands turned the page and lowered the newspaper.

A man with dark-grey flecked hair smoothed flat back over his head stared at Nat with surprise.

Nat tried to burrow into his soft seat. What was the man looking at?

The man continued to stare as he placed the newspaper on the seat beside him, and took a sheaf of papers in his hand.

"I suppose you know this is a first class carriage," he said, raising an eyebrow.

Nat took in a quick breath: "So— Sorry."

It had been on the tip of his tongue to say, "So what?" He would have argued with a stuffed shirt like that before, but he'd stopped himself in time. Toe the line. Don't draw attention to yourself.

"Sorry – didn't know," he repeated as he jumped to his feet.

He swung himself from seat to seat down the swaying carriage, through the door at the end, into a carriage packed with many more seats and no white linen seatbacks.

This was more like it. He should have guessed that the men in suits would be pampered on the train.

As he lowered himself into an empty seat, a hand tugged at his elbow.

"Here, dear. Look you can have my seat by the window. I'll move along."

Nat shrugged off the arm and found himself looking into the crinkled face of an old lady, grey hair rising in tight waves above her forehead, pink lipstick glistening among the powdery folds of her cheeks.

What did she want? Who was she?

Nat thought quickly. "Yep. I'll have the window."

He'd meant to sit on his own, but it might be better to pretend to be with the granny, to ward off trouble. He put his bag in the rack above, pushed past and sat down.

The old lady smiled, her eyes lighting up like the sparkly brooch on her coat.

"I always like company myself," she said. "You meet ever such nice people travelling. Live by myself, I do, since my dear Bill died, and I was always one for a bit of a chat, and now Bill's gone . . ." Her voice trailed away. She stared out of the window, and then back again. "Still, you don't want to hear about that now, do you, dear? Tell me about where you're going. No – let me guess!"

It was an effort. Nat didn't want to talk, but he told her about how he was going to visit his grandparents in Salisbury, and help his grandfather plant out his garden.

"You like gardening, do you? So did my Bill. Now tell me what you're going to plant?"

Nat racked his brains to think back to Mr Birt's allotment. "Broad beans," he said.

He looked around to see if there was another free seat. He'd had enough of all this questioning.

"Broad beans – lovely!" The hand tugged his arm again. "There's nothing like newly picked young broad beans – before they get too big and hard – in a bit of parsley sauce, with some rashers of smoked bacon and a handful of new potatoes soaking in butter."

Nat was starving. He hadn't thought to bring anything to eat, and she was going on about bacon.

"They say it's love that makes the world go round, but I say it's food."

She didn't stop. Each time Nat lapsed into silence, hoping for a bit of peace, she nudged his arm and started up again. She wanted his attention all the time.

The train had stopped twice since they had left the suburbs behind. Nat was terrified the old lady would distract him and he'd miss Salisbury. He kept glancing at his watch. Could she ... could she be deliberately trying to distract him, put him off his guard? He wasn't sure who to trust any longer. Spies everywhere, the girl had said.

"... never go out without my iron rations. Shocking food they serve up on these trains, at a price that's close to robbery."

She lifted a big black bag from beneath her feet and extracted a flask and a plastic box. Nat's nose twitched as she unscrewed the thermos lid and a tantalising smell of hot sweet tea met his nose. She poured a beaker for herself and then pulled out a second one.

"Always carry a spare. You don't know who you might want to share with," the old lady laughed. "Well, I think you've some lucky grandparents, a fine young man like you. I never had any children myself, so if they don't want you, you can ask them to lend you to me."

She laughed at her joke and handed Nat a mug. He couldn't resist it.

As he sipped the hot tea, the old lady pulled a newspaper from her bottomless bag and laid it flat on the table.

"Have a marmalade sandwich, dear," she said as she started munching. "Mmm ... look at that! I don't know what the world is coming to: little girl attacked in broad daylight, on that allotment. They don't know who she is either. And 'local boy is at present helping police with their enquiries'." The old lady tutted. "Poor lad. If he's done that he'll have it on his conscience all his life. One of those problem children, I expect."

Nat sat still, hardly daring to chew.

He was relieved when the door between the carriages slid back and the refreshments trolley rattled in.

Chapter Eight

"**S**HOCKING rubbish! I bought a Danish pastry from one of those trolleys last time, and, I declare, it must have been a good week old," said the old lady, leaning across Nat to peer at the trolley. She poked a finger at a bun wrapped in cellophane. "Sawdust!"

Nat was convinced the man in the black bow tie, pushing the trolley had heard, but he didn't give any sign of offence as he leant over the man in the seat across the aisle.

"And it's a scandal what they charge! I've a good mind to write to the head man, chief executive, or whatever nonsense they call them these days. It always pays to go to the top …"

The man turned towards them.

"Madam?" he said in a low voice.

"I'm not sure it's worth the money," sniffed the old lady. She pushed the buns aside and picked up a packet of biscuits. "I'll try these shortbreads – you can't do much to ruin shortbreads. And what about you, dear, I'll treat you to something tasty."

Nat chose a packet of biscuits and an orange juice. He had never had a granny and he was beginning to feel he'd missed something. He put out his hand for his drink. The train lurched and some juice slopped over.

"Give him a napkin," ordered the old lady, "or he'll be messing up his trousers."

"Certainly."

The waiter bent over the trolley, lifting packets and boxes and setting them back again. He didn't seem to know where the napkins were. Nat cringed with embarrassment at all the fuss.

"It's all right. It'll dry," he muttered.

"We seem to be out of napkins, madam."

"Out of napkins!" exclaimed the old lady. "Is this what you call service?"

Nat could have disappeared under the seat. He clutched the plastic cup so tight that it caved in again at the sides. The waiter must think he's a baby. He glanced up to find the man staring back with one dark eye. His other eye was half closed, hooded. Nat's hand clenched the cup, and he hardly felt the juice fall.

"Look at the mess you're making," said the old lady, pulling a tissue out of her sleeve.

As soon as the trolley moved on, Nat tried to get to his feet.

"Where are you off to?"

"I'm going to the gents."

"That's a good boy, you clean yourself up. What

are you taking your bag for?" she asked as she moved out of her seat to make room for him.

Nat pulled down his kit bag. His sleeping bag was bursting out. He pummelled it back in, wrenched the zip shut and slung it over his shoulder.

"I've got a flannel ..."

"You watch where you put things down, dear. These train toilets are none too clean."

Nat headed off in the opposite direction from that of the trolley, through the communicating door into the first-class compartment.

There weren't many people there: he'd be too conspicuous.

He hurried through First Class, past the man in the striped suit still writing on his papers, and sat down opposite a lady with yellow hair and scarlet fingernails. She looked over the glossy magazine she was reading. Nat could tell by her raised eyebrows what she was thinking. He sat there hot and sweating, with spilt juice down his sweat shirt, Craig's yellow *Daily Mail* cap knocked sideways.

"This seat isn't taken," he said defiantly. He didn't like her stare.

"No," she drawled, lifting her magazine as if to block him from view and pointedly pulling her navy handbag closer to her side. "No, I suppose not." Her voice was chilly from behind the magazine.

Nat was trying so hard to look casual that, for a minute, he didn't take in the distant rattling – the trolley was coming this way.

61

He struggled to his feet and dashed to the far end of the compartment. He turned the door handle but it wouldn't open. Locked. It was the back of the train and there were no more carriages.

As he turned round he met the eyes of the man in the striped suit. The man stood up and advanced towards him. The men in suits, the bad men?

"I think we have already established that you *were*" – the man spoke loudly, as if addressing the whole carriage – "and *are* not meant to be in First Class. I must insist you return to your correct carriage. First-class passengers have paid considerably more for their tickets to ensure peace and quiet. If you are looking for the lavatories you will no doubt find some in Second Class."

The lady with the magazine nodded in agreement, surveying Nat with distaste.

He was cornered. Were they in it with the waiter too? If the waiter with the trolley came into the carriage he would be trapped. The door at the end of the carriage was pulled back and the front wheels of a trolley pushed through.

Suddenly Nat lunged at the navy handbag perched by the woman on the seat. Clutching it tightly in his hands and displaying it high above his head, he lurched down the carriage.

"Stop him!" shrieked the woman. "Stop that boy! He's got my bag."

Nat collided with the trolley, kicking out, and pushing with his knees. Coffee and tea sprayed over the seats, a tower of plastic cups toppled and buns and biscuits rolled on to the floor.

"Look where you're— What do you think you're up to? Stop!" shouted the man behind the trolley, struggling to hold it upright. He was a small man with a black bow tie, a man with freckles and sandy red hair.

"Stop him! He's a thief!" the woman yelled. But the man was too short to reach Nat as he rushed past.

"Good Lord!" cried the man in the pinstriped suit. "The thug! Broad daylight, in First Class!"

"I don't know, sir, I don't know what's going on. There's a gang of them, aboard, sir. First my trolley disappears, then the lady has her handbag snatched ..."

Nat left the voices behind as he swayed through the second-class carriage as slowly as he dared, swinging the handbag overhead. Passengers stared curiously until they suddenly realised what was happening.

At last an alarm bell started ringing!

He had been afraid he'd have to brave the next carriage before the alarm was set off.

"Catch him!"

"I'll get him!"

"Oh, darling, sit down. He might have a knife."

"Where's the guard, for heaven's sake?"

"Mobile phone, that's what we need. Go and see if there's someone in First Class with a mobile phone."

"I warned you trains are dangerous nowadays. I'm never coming—"

Nat shut out the shouting as he slipped through the

door marked Toilet. He locked the door and stood there shaking as the train ground to a halt.

The window was frosted glass, but open at the top. Nat stood on the lavatory seat and peered out. Several men in railway uniforms were running along beside the train, then he heard footsteps and shouting in the corridor.

"He ran through!" yelled a man.

"Couldn't stop him – he had a knife."

The door handle turned. "Who's in here, please?" A sharp knocking rang against the door.

Nat sucked in his breath. "Out in a minute," he said in a high squeaky voice.

"Sorry, madam. Just checking."

Whoever it was moved away. Nat dropped the handbag on the floor, hoisted up his kit bag and opened the door. With sweaty hands he pulled down the window on the passage door, pulled himself up on the window ledge, wriggled through and lowered his feet to the track. Then he somersaulted into the lush undergrowth lining the steep bank that fell away from the railway line.

He lay still, his chest heaving with the thudding deep inside.

"I'm sure I saw someone jump out," called a deep voice.

Several men in uniform and one in a striped suit passed within a few feet at the top of the embankment.

"No, sir, there's no one here. Look, all the doors

are closed. Must have been our men you saw, inspecting the train."

"I'm convinced someone leapt out in a hurry."

"Know what I think, sir? Bet you anything that boy is still on this train. He'll be in a toilet, most like, but we've got the police coming aboard at the next station. There's more than one of this gang about, so we'd best get moving so that the police can sort them out."

Doors slammed, the train started to creak, then edged slowly along the track.

Nat shivered with fright. Itchy pains bit into his arms. He tried to scratch, but grasped instead a fistful of nettles. He didn't dare move. He might not have been the only one to leave the train.

They were after him for sure. They knew he had the envelope. Whatever those papers were about they must be worth a lot.

He heaved a shuddering sigh. They had him up against the ropes now and he'd never been so frightened in his life. Surely the best thing would be to chuck away the envelope, where they could find it. He wasn't enjoying being followed, never knowing when the blow would come.

He could make out a muddy ditch at the foot of the embankment. Above its brown sheen, flies swarmed across the surface. What if he tore the paper and envelope into little pieces and dropped them in the ditch? They would soon disintegrate and disappear.

But what good was that? Even if he got rid of the envelope, they'd never let him go now, not while he knew who had attacked the girl.

But would anyone believe him? Would Mr Prendergast, the police, or Mum, for that matter, believe him? He couldn't prove he had nothing to do with the attack on the little girl, and there was so much evidence assembled against him.

"And snatching handbags from ladies on trains as well!" He could already hear Mr Prendergast's rumbling voice.

No – there wasn't a choice: he had to bounce back, defences ready. He'd find Professor Keeping, and see if he knew who could have been after Dr Buxton and her girl.

The wind rustled the branches of the bush beside him. In the distance he heard sheep bleating. How could it sound so peaceful when life was such a mess?

He lifted his head. Fields stretched out for miles and miles. The embankment ran down to a field sprouting some sort of crop. Another field beyond was dotted with grey sheep and beyond that he could see a large brick barn. On hands and knees he crawled down to the ditch.

He sat with his chin sunk on his knees. What was he going to do? He had no idea where he was, but he reckoned from his watch that he was over halfway to Salisbury.

He'd have to wait until he was sure no one was about.

He wasn't used to the country. All this empty space and quiet and damp. No – he clenched his fist – no one was going to get him to that prison school in the country!

He'd nearly made an awful mess of it, but from now on he would be ready with his footwork – on guard.

Chapter Nine

NAT DIDN'T dare move away from the bottom of the embankment. He had to be sure no one had jumped out after him. He spent most of the day sitting in the undergrowth with his back to a small tree, listening to the trains thundering past above him. It was frustrating knowing that most of them were going to Salisbury, but there was no way he could board one.

The shadows began to lengthen and the air grew colder.

It must be after tea by now, he thought. There would be fewer people about, so he ought to be moving on.

Nat edged round the ploughed field and was skirting the hedge of the sheep field, when he heard the drone. It didn't sound like a plane and it wasn't a helicopter, so it couldn't be the police.

A black splodge hovered clumsily, flying low over the tree tops. Like a drunken bluebottle it zig-zagged backwards and forwards, crossing the railway line and over the fields. Nat ducked into the hedge; he had never seen anything like it before.

As the splodge grew closer, it looked a bit like a flying bicycle. Nat could make out a helmeted and goggled figure, open to the air but sitting back in the machine.

A microlite, that's what it was! He'd seen one in a book of modern flying machines at school.

Nat dived deeper into the hedge as the microlite circled round and round above him.

Young lambs squealed with fright and rushed bleating to their mothers. The sheep charged first one way, then another, to escape the insistent drone. Suddenly the microlite executed a turn, and flew off, back the way it had come, skimming the tree tops.

Could the pilot have spotted him? Would the microlite have gone on circling so long above him if the pilot hadn't seen something?

He had to hide before the machine came back.

Nat stumbled round the hedge, making for the brick barn he could see in the distance. As he got near he found that it lay on the edge of a dip or shallow valley. Two hundred metres or so below was a farm surrounded by outbuildings.

It wasn't ideal, but it was shelter. Nat had thought the barn stood on its own, not close to people who might see him; but he needed somewhere to hide, to get out of the cold and plan his next move.

He slipped through the massive wooden doors wedged slightly ajar. The barn was huge. Its roof arched with great wooden beams. Bales of straw were stacked almost to the ceiling and a long metal ladder was propped against them right to the top.

Nat climbed the ladder and found a hollow where some bales had already been pulled out. It was like a cave in there, warm and dark and inviting.

He slumped on the straw, opened his bag and pulled out his thick Oxfam sweater. Along with the sweater tumbled out the old lady's plastic lunch box. In his haste he must have packed it when he zipped up his bag on the train. He tore it open. There was a small carton of orange juice with a straw, a sardine sandwich neatly wrapped in clingfilm, a tomato and an apple.

Nat was starving; he'd missed out on lunch. Normally he didn't like sardines, and he wasn't too keen on tomatoes for that matter, but this evening they tasted delicious. Nat wolfed the lot, but he was still hungry.

And he was terribly tired.

He was exhausted by the day: out late last night at the shed, the early start for the station, the terrifying journey. He spread out the thick sweater in the hollow between the two bales and was asleep in minutes.

The shrill voice dragged Nat awake. He wanted to sleep; it was dark and he was so tired, but the voice didn't let up.

"Friend or enemy?"

"Ugh ... what?"

"You've got to do it properly! Friend or enemy?"

A beam of light shone into Nat's face, blinding him as he dragged his eyes open.

"Put that torch down. I can't see."

"But you haven't answered me ..."

Nat was wide awake now. It was a child's voice.

Nat lunged towards the torch. The light retreated and Nat fell on his face in the straw.

"Watch out! You'll dislodge the bales and then we'll both fall down. What are you doing here?"

It was only a kid, Nat thought scornfully as he pulled himself up. His instinct was to shove him out of the way, and make off, but he couldn't do that. The boy might run and tell his parents. He had to be careful, keep the boy talking, play up to him until he could get away.

"I'm a friend," Nat muttered through gritted teeth.

"No – never!" said the boy. "I guessed you might be a friendly agent, but I had to check first."

Was this kid mad or something?

"Who sent you? Where are you from?" The boy's eager face came in close to Nat.

Nat stared back in disbelief.

"Honest, you can trust me. Cross my heart and hope to die."

"OK," said Nat slowly.

"I know all about secrets. I've read about spying in my book, about how they used children as agents, so the enemy would never suspect them. Are you carrying a secret message?"

71

"What's it to you?" said Nat. Did the boy know something or was he playing some little kid's make-believe game?

"Sorry," giggled the boy. "I shouldn't ask questions. Don't worry: you can trust me."

The boy set the torch down on an overhead bale. Nat could see him now in the beam. He was a couple of years younger than Nat, with ginger hair springing out from under a brown woolly hat. A matching brown knitted scarf was swathed round his neck, and he was wearing a big, patched, green sweater. He leant towards Nat, his eyes glittering with excitement in the torchlight.

"It's all right – I'm not going to ask you what it is, or who it's for. I mean it's got to be a secret if you're an agent, hasn't it?"

"Yeah, that's right."

"I've read all about agents and the secret service. I knew it was only a matter of time before I met one."

The boy must be nuts.

"It's dead boring here: nothing ever happens, but being right next to army land I knew if I watched and waited something was bound to happen. I mean someone has got to be after our military secrets, haven't they?"

"Where's here exactly?" said Nat slowly. "I ... I lost my map."

"You didn't lose it! Agents never lose things ..."

"You can't help it if you're being chased," said Nat. He couldn't stand other kids criticising him, even if it was make-believe. "I had to jump off a train."

72

"Off a train? Wow! And you're not hurt? It's Kung Fu, isn't it, falling without hurting?"

Nat was glad Sean and Adam weren't around. It was beneath him making up to a boy as stupid as this. But he had to keep his irritation tied down: the boy might be able to ...

"Where exactly ...?"

"Little Whittington, that's where the farm is, my dad's farm."

"Anywhere near Salisbury?" Nat tried to sound casual, friendly even.

"There's a bus twice a week to Salisbury, for market day. It takes about an hour because you collect people from lots of villages on the way. But" – the boy's face screwed up in a worried look – "you haven't told me whose side you're on."

What was the kid going on about?

"I'm English, aren't I?"

The boy grinned with relief.

"I thought you probably were. I couldn't hear a foreign accent. But who's after you? The Russians aren't interested any longer. Dad says they're friendly now, but I think there are Communists still ..."

The boy gabbled on as if expecting Nat to be interested in his political lecture. But the boy had something. Who would want to spy on the army now? Nat hadn't a clue.

" 'Fraid it's confidential. Can't give away secret information."

"Of course not," agreed the boy. "Real agents never

73

would. I shouldn't have asked. Sorry!"

"But you can help me, if you're not scared," said Nat.

"Scared?" the boy gulped. "Me? Course I'm not scared. Can I really help you?"

Nat nodded. "Just like in the books. I'll need a map, and you can draw me a plan of how to find the bus to Salisbury. Then you've got to keep quiet about me, or –" Nat paused and lowered his voice to a hiss – "it could be a very messy business for you."

The boy adjusted the scarf on his neck.

"Oh yes! I understand. I won't let you down."

"Well then," Nat tried a smile, "I could do with a bit more food."

"We'll need a password, won't we?"

"Just get the map—"

"But we have to have a password, do things properly."

"OK, OK," said Nat racking his brains. " 'Allotment'."

"What's an allotment?"

"You just do what you're told and stop the questions," Nat's voice had started to rise.

"Of course, I forgot. Agents always obey orders, don't they?" The boy was bouncing his torch up and down with excitement. "But we've got to have agent names so no one knows our identity."

This was turning into a comedy show. He was never going to get rid of the boy if they kept up like this all night. At this rate they could have written their own spy story by the morning.

"I'm ..." Nat racked his brains. "... I'm Ace and you're ... You're—"

"Zero!" whooped the boy. "How about that – I'll be Zero!"

"Now look here, Zero," said Nat with fury. "Keep your voice down and no questions, you understand? Your mission is to get me food, a map, and help me on to the bus to Salisbury."

"Mission understood, Ace," said the boy solemnly. He backed away until his woollen hat had disappeared down the ladder.

Nat yawned and stretched. He didn't think he was going to get any decent sleep at this rate until the whole mess was sorted out. What time was it, anyway?

He looked at his watch: 11.30.

Suddenly Nat was wide awake. What was that boy doing in the barn, fully dressed with a torch, on a school night, at 11.30? That game with the spies: surely the boy hadn't meant it? Perhaps he had been sent to take Nat in, to spy out where Nat was.

And he could be telling them now.

He'd been a fool, Nat realised as he pushed the sandwich box back in his bag, crammed in the sweater he'd been lying on, and pulled the zip.

Beneath him someone coughed. Then he heard a rustle, as if straw was being displaced.

He wasn't alone in the barn. There was someone else there too, down below, on the floor. If he went down the ladder he'd be trapped. Why had he spent so long nattering on to that ridiculous boy? It could only have been deliberate, to keep Nat occupied and unaware while someone moved into place beneath them.

Nat stared frantically around him. Above him he could make out the black bar of a crossbeam; it seemed to run to the other side of the roof. If he could swing along it and drop down the other side ...

The torch was still on! He must be visible in its beam.

Nat reached up for the torch and swung its beam round, then rolled it to the far side of the bales. With any luck whoever was watching below would think he had moved across.

Nat had his hands on the cobwebby beam when the dark outline of the boy appeared in the barn door.

"Ace?" whispered the boy urgently. "Ace! Are you still up there? It's all right, it's me – Zero."

No – he'd never make it along the beam now. The boy had one foot on the ladder already, and he was carrying something.

"I've got some cold sausages and bread and a piece of Mum's fruit cake. Ace, where are you?"

Nat panicked. He could be trapped within minutes. The ladder – it was the only way out.

"Mum will be mad in the morning. She says she always knows when I've been helping myself to cake. I ate a whole cake once, I couldn't stop ... Hey, Ace, what are you doing? Watch out!"

Nat dropped down the ladder. The boy was in his

76

way. Nat tried to jump past him but his ankle caught in a rung and he crashed to the hard floor.

"Ace! Watch out!" the boy scrambled on to the dirt floor beside Nat. "Now the sausage and cake will be all dirty. I thought agents were meant to know how to fall. I mean coming down a ladder should be a piece of cake ..." The boy stopped and giggled. "Cake – do you get it? Funny, isn't it?" The boy held out a sweet-smelling spicy handful. "Cake, see. Good one that."

Nat's thigh and leg hurt. This boy was stupid, really stupid ... or ... he was a good actor.

No. He was too stupid to be acting. But even if he always went in for these pretend games, that still didn't explain what he was doing here at this hour. Nat's mum couldn't do much with him, but even he wouldn't dare stay out until 11.30 and not let her know where he was.

Where were the boy's parents? What were they thinking of?

The boy was dusting off the sausages and cake and laying them out on a straw ledge.

"Where's the torch, Ace? We need the torch."

Who was in charge here? Nat felt an overwhelming desire to give the boy a sharp punch, show him who was boss. That's what he'd have done in playground at school if one of the younger boys had shown him such lip.

Hold in the punch, he said to himself. Think tactics.

He needed the boy on his side.

"Get it yourself, Zero," said Nat through clenched teeth. "What's that you've got under your arm?"

"Bottles," said the boy, setting down three pointed shapes. "I'll get the torch then." And he began to climb the ladder.

Nat picked up one of the dark shapes. It was warm, and – he couldn't believe it – it was a baby's bottle with a rubber teat, and there were three of them.

Then, behind him, came that cough again.

Chapter Ten

"WHAT's that?" whispered Nat.

"What d'you say, Ace?" came the boy's voice as he started down the ladder with the torch.

Nat couldn't see the boy clearly, but he could see the beam flashing through the dark as he stepped down each rung.

"There's someone here?"

"Is there?" said the boy in an excited whisper. "Where?"

From behind them came the rustle of straw again.

"There! Who have you brought with you?" demanded Nat fiercely, grabbing his bag, a plan of escape already forming in his mind.

The boy giggled. "Not Scraggy? It's Scraggy. Haven't you seen him? Look, over in the pen."

Nat followed the boy and the torch beam over to the pen at the far side of the barn. In the yellow torchlight a wet black nose sniffled up at them in a pale woolly face framed with dark, floppy ears. The little black mouth opened, and a grating cough burst out.

Nat stared into the tiny pink mouth and throat quaking with each cough.

"Is it a lamb?" he said in amazement.

The lamb tottered over to the boy on knobbly black legs and nuzzled his hand. Nat had never seen anything so pretty and vulnerable.

"What's it doing here? Why isn't it out in the field with the others?"

"He's my lamb. Dad had given up on him. He said I could have him, but only if I looked after him all myself. He was dying ... but he's getting better."

"Dying?"

"Dad found him under a hedge. Dad reckons he was one of triplets and the ewe didn't have enough milk for three, and as he was the weakest and smallest, he got left out."

The lamb's black tail flicked in the air, but it soon fell back as its woolly head shook with a cough.

"What's it make that noise for?" said Nat. "They're meant to bleat, aren't they?"

"You should have heard him yesterday ... sounded as rough as an old tractor engine! I think he's got a bit of pneumonia. I gave him a shot of penicillin this morning and he's already much better. Look, he's got an appetite."

The boy took one of the baby's bottles and climbed into the pen. The lamb rushed at the bottle, tugging at the teat for all it was worth, black tail flying in the air.

"Is that why you're here – because of the lamb?"

"Dad said if I took on the lamb I was responsible for it, so I've got to get up and feed him in the night until he's bigger and stronger."

"Is that why ... ?"

"You were lying just where I was going to put my sleeping bag. That was really lucky, Ace; I've always wanted to meet a spy." The boy grinned at Nat as if he was having the time of his life. "It's been the best week ever: Dad gave me my first orphan lamb to look after, and I've met a spy, and I—"

"I wouldn't get up every night for a lamb," said Nat scornfully, but he knew he would – he would give anything to have a lamb to look after. "You're going to get up all through the night to feed it?"

"I have to ... he might die if I don't. If he gets any worse I'm going to put the heat lamp on him." The boy pointed to a lamp hanging down over the pen. "Old Pete, the pigman, is coming in to check and feed Scraggy when I'm at school. But at night it gets really cold: I've got to sleep here until he's stronger, but I think he's mending already," he added proudly.

The boy had seemed such a little boy playing ridiculous spy games, but now he seemed years older than Nat. To have to take responsibility for another life, get up all through the night ... Nat had left the girl. She had wanted him to stay, but he'd tried to get rid of her and left her. He hadn't wanted that responsibility; no thank you.

"Have a sausage – they're yummy," said the boy. "I

81

couldn't find a map, so I tore a page out of Dad's road atlas in the car. He'll be furious with me if he finds out!"

"And the bus?" said Nat.

"You're lucky – tomorrow is market day in Salisbury. The bus leaves outside the village shop at eight-thirty."

"But how ... ?"

"There's only one way. You follow the track from the farm until it reaches the lane. Turn towards the big sycamores and after five minutes you come into the village."

"Which street is the village shop in?"

The boy giggled. "There's only one street in the village and one shop. You can't miss it – Bakery Stores, there's a sign outside."

Nat pondered. It seemed easy enough. He'd have to make sure he was awake early enough to watch the time. Then he remembered the track he had seen meandering up from the farm to the barn. It ran through a field with no hedges to conceal it.

"I might be seen on the track."

"No. You'll be safe. There's only Mum and Dad to see you, and it's Mum's egg day at the market. Dad drives her there early to set up the stall. She cooks my breakfast and leaves straight after, and that's quite a bit before the market bus leaves from the village. When they've gone, you can leave."

Nat thought it over. No one knew he was in the barn, apart from the boy. There'd been the microlite, but Nat hadn't moved until it had gone away. If he could get to the bus and hide among the other passengers he should be safe.

The boy's eyes looked up from the lamb to Nat. "You can count on me, Ace. I haven't seen anyone. It's really boring round here: we never see anyone new, so I'd have noticed a stranger a mile off. I've been watching every bit of the farm for ages and ages; you see I've been practising a long time with my spying books for this."

Nat pulled out his sleeping bag. He and the boy set up a sleeping station in the hollow in the straw bales, their sleeping bags pulled well back from the edge. If anyone came into the barn, they would hear intruders before they could be seen.

The boy set up an alarm clock between them. Nat sank into his soft sleeping bag. The straw beneath him smelt like the sportsfield on a hot summer's day, when the groundsman had mown it. Nat breathed in the fresh warm smell and was asleep.

The alarm went off in the middle of the night. The boy disappeared down the ladder. Nat heard him moving around below, and a rough cough and a rustling.

Nat was warm in his bag. Don't you dare wake me, he thought in his half sleep. Don't bother me.

The next thing he knew the boy was slumped down beside him, back in his sleeping bag and asleep, snoring gently. Nat liked the snoring, the warmth in the hollow of hay beneath him, and the dusty, grassy smells around him. He liked the feeling of togetherness.

The alarm woke him again. On and on it went.

"Get that alarm off," rasped Nat. "Get it off. Someone is going to hear it."

The boy muttered and went on sleeping.

"Come on," said Nat, sitting up. "You don't have to wake me too, with your stupid sheep."

The boy stirred, groaned and went back to sleep.

Nat reached for the alarm button. He should wake the boy, but he was obviously knackered after getting up all the night before. The kid had to wake in time in the morning if Nat was to get away ... He didn't want the boy's parents coming to look for him.

Slowly an idea took shape in his mind, an idea that brought a delighted smile to his face.

Nat crawled out of his sleeping bag, torch in hand, and set his bare feet carefully and silently on the ladder. He held on to the edge of the ladder and surveyed the shimmering scene beneath him. The door of the barn was still ajar and an eerie, silvered light swept the floor, punctured only by the narrow beam of the torch. Below him he could make out the black outline of the pen, and hear the lamb snuffling and moving around. Nat shivered, and climbed slowly down the ladder.

Two of the three bottles next to the pen were empty now. Nat picked up the last full one and climbed into the pen. The lamb sniffed his hand suspiciously.

Nat tipped the bottle up and a couple of drops fell on the lamb's black nose. Then Scraggy grabbed the teat and tugged. Nat was amazed how hard the little animal could pull on the teat. He could hear the milk spurting into the lamb's throat and its noisy gulps. Its whole body wiggled with delight, its black tail waving in the air.

Gradually the milk sank down in the bottle. All that milk in the lamb, and he, Nathan Price, had given it!

"There, Scraggy. All right now?" he said. He put out his hand and rubbed the warm wriggling back. He was surprised how thick and tight the lamb's wool coat was. He could feel bones sticking through the wool. The boy had said the lamb would soon fatten up, if it had the milk regularly.

Nat watched as the lamb licked its lips, dropped down on front legs, curled round its back legs, tucked its nose down in the warm straw and closed its eyes.

He stood there staring at it and then switched off the torch. In the silver light he climbed back up the ladder.

"What time is it? Have I ...?" The boy sat up suddenly.

"It's all right," said Nat. "I've fed Scraggy."

"You fed him! Did he take the bottle all right?"

"Yes – the lot."

The boy flopped back asleep. Nat lay there a while, thinking of the lamb's warm, compact, squirming body. It was all quiet below. The lamb was asleep.

Nat woke to the boy's tread as he climbed down the ladder. The barn was filled with a cold grey light.

Nat sat up. He was warm in his sleeping bag and he

85

longed to stay sheltered in the barn. But the cold daylight picked out the muck and dirt on his hands.

No, there was a real world out there, one he couldn't hide from any longer, and he had to get going.

A red school exercise book and a pencil lay open beside him. It seemed to be a record of the times Scraggy had been fed and a record of a penicillin injection. Beside the 3 a.m. slot, the boy had written 'ACE – 1 botal.' Beneath it a note was scribbled.

'Have gone for brekfast, listen for van leeving and go, and thanks for feeding Scraggy, good luck Zero.'

Nat's confidence wavered now he realised he was on his own again. He liked the barn. He would like to have stayed and helped look after Scraggy, and to have slept in the warm hay again. He wanted to hear more about looking after sheep.

And the boy was a friendly kid. Most little kids were frightened of him, but this boy had chatted away happily. But he hadn't dared come on heavy with him; he'd needed the boy's help too much.

He was worried. Where was he going to now? Where would it all end? Come to think of it, if *he* was worried, Mum would be in a right state by now.

Nat took the stubby pencil and turned to the next page in the exercise book.

'Zero,' he scribbled rapidly. *'Post this in an envelope as soon as you can to Mrs Price, 3H, Jubilee Block, Wentworth Mansions ...'*

Then he tore off a bit of paper and wrote:

86

'I'm OK, Mum. Don't worry. I've got to find some-one. He may know about the girl, then you will know it wasn't me.'

Nat looked in his dinner-money store and found two twenty pence pieces. He wedged them into the exercise book to pay for the stamp, and then he left the book beside the pen, where the boy would find it.

Nat wearily packed his sleeping bag into his kit bag and put on his scratchy sweater. He chewed half a sausage he found in the straw and climbed down the ladder to the barn door.

Outside the sky was grey and heavy. A fine drizzle had coated the new grass with a shiny wetness and had made the hard mud ruts outside the barn slimy. It was seven-thirty. Any minute the boy's parents would set out.

Nat leant in the doorframe and watched the farm beneath him.

He didn't have to wait long before a man came out in a hat and mac, followed by a shorter woman with a scarf tied round her head. The man went round the back of the outbuildings and returned driving a van. The woman was scurrying backwards and forwards carrying trays and shouting back into the house.

"... school bus," drifted up to Nat, and, "Don't be late!"

Then the woman stopped, tray in her arms, and stared down the track leading to the lane. Like some fat black beetle, a sleek black car was making its way up the track to the farm.

Nat's mouth tasted bitter. That wasn't a country car. That was an expensive city car.

So they had known all along where he was! The microlite pilot had seen him.

Nat edged back behind the doorframe and watched. The boy's parents, and the boy himself stood awaiting the car's arrival. Bumpily it made its way along the rutted track and stopped beside the van. A man in a dark suit got out and put up a large black umbrella.

For a time the little group seemed to be talking among themselves. Then the man went back to the car and got out a flash of something pale. He spread open a newspaper and showed it to the group. The boy's father took the paper, then lowered it to show his son, and the whole group bent in a huddle around the boy.

As if on puppet strings, the group turned and stared at the barn and then back to the car, where a second man in black was getting out.

Nat didn't wait. He had to get away.

He slung his bag over his back and slipped to the ground, beside the barn. On his hands and knees he crawled over the muddy ruts, across acres of wet grass, to a sheltering hedge. He was hot, burning, despite the drizzle. Wide awake now, his heart pounding in his ears, he ran doubled over, stumbling up the hill.

Chapter Eleven

N AT'S BACK ached. He had to keep down, keep to the line of the hedge.

But he should get through the hedge and run along the far side, so that they wouldn't be able to see him.

Nat examined the dense barrier, packed with prickly thorns. Then he glanced down the hill and saw the little group moving over from the farmhouse to the barn, with the smaller figure of Zero leading them.

Rotten little twerp! You couldn't trust anyone but yourself, and he'd been a fool to think otherwise.

Beneath the hedge Nat stumbled on a gaping hole, spilling fresh earth. It looked like the entrance to some animal burrow.

He scraped frantically at the loose earth, cupping his hands like a trowel. The hole widened into a muddy channel beneath the hedge. Flattening himself, he squeezed painfully forward.

The cold and wet seeped through to his T-shirt, threads tugged and ripped in his sweater, and sharp spikes dug into his skin. His eyes began to water. *Go on.* He was through.

Above him rough grassland stretched to the top of the hill. Bent over, Nat ran along the hedge, following the contours of the hill. He must be above the farm.

He kept going until he came to a rough cart track. A deep breath shuddered through him as he stopped to calm his panting and listen.

No drones, no car noises, no threatening shouts.

Slowly he stood up. Nestled beneath the hill, at the bottom of the valley, a church spire rose up above a cluster of shining roofs. It had to be the village. Then, as he watched, a green bus chugged into view, winding slowly down a hilly lane on the far side of the village.

The market bus! The bus to Salisbury ...

Nat raced down the track, slipping and sliding on the slimy ruts. He had to get on that bus before Zero led the men to the barn and they worked out which way he had headed.

The men in suits: they were clever. Even if the microlite hadn't seen him get to the barn, they had worked out where he was. But surely they wouldn't dare ... ? They couldn't force him off a public bus.

Nat skidded down the track. It stopped at the lane. He turned towards the village, running past a tiny school playground and along the village street.

There was no one about. No one waiting for the market bus.

Above him a sign creaked, 'Bakery Stores'. The

glass of the door beneath was covered with a torn
poster:

EASTER BARN DANCE
to the bopping beat of the
RAY BUNTING QUINTET!

Where was the bus? Nat had to find out where the
stop was.

He tried the door and a bell rang deep inside the
shop. A man, with a red face above a tightly knotted tie
that was edging his collar up to his chin, looked up
from the till, and beamed at Nat.

"Good morning!" he said. He rubbed his hands and
bent over the counter towards Nat. "Bit chilly again,
isn't it," he added, as if sharing some secret. "Not such
a pleasant morning as we've been having of late." He
leant back, his hands fingering his tie knot, and looked
Nat up and down. "And what can I do for you, young
man?"

Nat was suddenly aware of his wet muddy clothes,
the torn threads on his sweater, and his breath belching
out like a steam engine.

"The bus ..." Nat gasped. "Where can I get the
bus?"

"The market bus?" said the man, eyeing Nat curiously. "Well, lad, you've missed that for sure. In fact,"
he held up his wrist to check his watch. "You've missed
it by one and a quarter minutes precisely. What a
shame! And it looks as if you've had quite a run ...
Come far?"

91

Nat gasped in a deep breath, speechless.

What was he going to do? The men would come looking for him within minutes. If they came, they'd ask for him, he was sure of that. He had to get out, hide.

"I'm – I'm going to walk to the station."

"Station? Where you trying to get to?"

"London." All trains went to London, didn't they?

"Ah, the London train," the man nodded slowly. "Walking to the station, are you then?"

"Yes. Is it far?"

"Far ... yes," said the man, staring at Nat. "I mean – no!" He bent over the till, pulled out a roll of paper and examined it intently. "Just follow the road straight out of the village," he said, unfurling a length of roll. "Keep walking, along the lane, straight ahead. You've got plenty of time for the train. Just straight ahead. Don't turn off, and you'll come to it."

"How far?" demanded Nat.

He'd have to catch another train to get away from this place.

"Oh, forty ... forty-five minutes." The man's cheery interest seemed to have faded fast enough; but then most grown-ups gave up on him pretty quick.

"I'll have a paper – and a cola, and this Bounty Bar," said Nat sullenly.

"Certainly," said the man.

He folded the paper slowly and deliberately and handed it to Nat.

Nat jumped as a bell clanged above his head. An

old lady limped in, leaning on a walking stick. A decrepit dog, with hanging head, staggered in behind her.

"I'll have my usual loaf and a packet of tea, Harry," she said. "Weather's turned, hasn't it? Winter's back ..."

Nat took his chance and slipped out of the shop.

What was he going to do? He could make for the station straight away, or lie low for a while. But the station was such an obvious place to head for. If he hid he could check that the black car had gone. He really wanted to run, get away from this place, but he had to control himself, think it out ...

No – he couldn't outrun the men in suits. They were clever, so he had to be clever, use his brain, keep calm.

He was frightened, but a new feeling rose in him, a feeling he wasn't used to: a calmness, confidence even.

Yes, he was still on his feet; they hadn't knocked him down. He was ready for another bout.

He headed back the way he had come and climbed the first gate he saw. It led into a field dotted with curved arches of rusty corrugated iron, penned in with bales of straw. Around the pens crowds of tiny pink pigs were running and squealing, or sucking at the teats of muddy sows wallowing on their sides in the dirt. The place stank, but he didn't have any choice.

He made for one of the pens. It was empty. Nat hauled himself in and lay there, peering out. The field sloped up and, at the top, he could make out the red brick wall of the farm.

He was just in time. Bumping along the track at the side of the field was the sleek black car.

It purred slowly down the track, stopped at the lane, and then accelerated with a roar into the village.

Nat kept his eyes on the road leading out of the village, up the hill on the far side. No car appeared. After about ten minutes a cattle truck went up the hill. Then suddenly there was a roar and puff of exhaust smoke and Nat saw the black beetle whizz up the hill.

Nat sat back against the bales, slapped his thigh and grinned. Whoever was in that car had been told that Nat was heading for the station.

Nat crawled back under the half-moon of iron, pulled out his newspaper and made himself comfortable against his kit bag. He pulled the can ring on his cola and tore the paper off the Bounty Bar.

His teeth bit into the sweet white coconut. He chewed, took a drink, and then spread out the paper.

Nothing on the front. All a lot of scandal about some politician taking money he shouldn't have – as if anyone was surprised! Good stuff on the football at the back; even got Rombridge in the third league. What was he missing on telly tonight? A bit of horror: *Abandon the Living*. He hadn't seen that one. Really chilly, Sean had said.

He gripped the page and stared. It was huge, the black and white photograph staring out at him. It was like staring into a mirror image of himself.

He couldn't believe it! His stupid school photograph.

Mum had insisted on cutting his hair before it was taken, but at least he had made his mark, wearing his shirt with the fraying collar and his tie pulled down.

Underneath, in bold black writing:

IS THIS THE FACE OF A KILLER?

Nat didn't know how long he sat there, numb and cold. Had the girl died?

He'd been called such a load of rubbish in recent years: a bully, lazy, school cutter, thief. He had pretended he didn't care at first and then gradually he had got used to it and let it roll off him.

But it was all true.

He deserved it, but he didn't care any longer what people thought, except Mum of course. He tried to look after Mum and she knew. She had never said he was bad.

But a killer ... Surely no one could believe that of him. It wasn't possible that people could believe that of him!

The man in the shop, the man who had given him the paper, he hadn't asked for the money, nor the money for the Bounty Bar. Nat hadn't meant to go off without paying. He'd forgotten in his panic, and the man had forgotten too ...

But the shopkeeper had taken his time telling him how to get to the station ...

Nat grabbed his kit bag and up-ended it on the ground. The torn map was there, the page Zero had torn out of his father's road atlas. Nat smoothed out the creases with his sticky hand.

What had Zero said the village was called? Little Whittington – that was it.

Nat placed a shaking finger on the black dot that was Salisbury, and traced back the black line of the railway.

There was no station anywhere near Little Whittington. The next station was miles back, over the other side of the page ... And the road leading out of Little Whittington towards Salisbury, it wasn't even a red or green road, just a little white road wiggling between villages. It didn't go anywhere near the railway line.

Chapter Twelve

HE HAD to think. He'd been rushing to find this Professor Keeping at Lower Ebbsbourne, thinking he'd make it easily in a day, but it was Friday already. The congress started tomorrow.

The shop owner had spotted him; he'd tried to trap Nat with false directions. He'd probably told the men in the black car too, as they had shot out of the village in such a hurry.

Whoever was in that car wanted Nat before the police found him.

Zero wouldn't be any use now. No wonder the kid had shopped him, with the IS THIS THE FACE OF A KILLER? school photo.

Nat shivered. The Oxfam sweater smelt musty with damp. His legs and back ached. He should rest, move on at night.

He laid his sleeping bag out on the mud floor beneath the rusty iron roof. If he kept down behind the

97

bales no one would guess he was there, stuck in a muddy sea of squealing pigs.

He was so tired. He closed his eyes and dozed.

There was Mum: "I've lost the key, Nat." Mum was struggling to close the stiff front door. "I'm sure I put it in my basket." Mum was scrabbling in her bag. She couldn't find it. The bag fell, spilling its contents on the concrete walkway. "It's not here, Nat ..." Mum's voice was breaking with tears. She turned to plead with Nat, "Have you got it, Nat? What am I going to do ...?"

Nat reached out to help, to touch his mother, but his hand was full of spiky straw.

He felt groggy and stiff, his clothes damp and dirty. He had been asleep for ages. Heavy grey clouds still coated the sky, but the drizzle had stopped.

Nat heard the insistent toot; so that was what had woken him.

Peering over a bale, he saw a white smudge near the clump of trees at the bottom of the drive.

A white car ... It tooted again as a small car, bright yellow against the muddy brown of the field, chugged into view down the lane. Ambrose Prendergast!

And the white car...! Nat watched it turn up the track, a red stripe along the side – a police car tooting to indicate the turning up to the farm. The shopkeeper, or Zero's parents, must have called the police.

For a moment Nat was overcome by an irresistible urge to rush out shouting across the field, to hail Mr

Prendergast. His was a familiar face after all, and that huge chest seemed so solid and reliable; surely, he would believe Nat, if Nat told him he hadn't touched the girl.

No, Nat thought in disgust, don't get soft. Why should Mr Prendergast believe him when nobody else ever did?

Nothing had changed. He had to push on or he was down and out; he wasn't ready to be counted out yet. He'd get to Salisbury somehow, even if it meant walking through the night.

A third car, a black shiny car, was turning into the track.

Nat's mouth was dry, and there was a pain in his neck as he peered over the bales. So the men in black had guessed he hadn't got away, that he was still around. They were clever enough to look over at the pig shelters and put two and two together.

The black car turned in under the trees. It drove in so deep behind a holly bush that Nat could no longer see it.

Then two dark figures emerged from behind the holly bush. They separated and each climbed a gate into the fields bordering the track. Nat could see the one in the pig field, running up inside the hedge. They were heading for the farm and they didn't want anyone to know.

But he knew … The police were on his tail now as well as the men in black, and they were horribly close. He had to get moving. But where to?

Then a crazy, mad idea flushed through him, and he quickly stuffed his things into his bag.

"Come on ahead, have you? Get in, son. You look as if you've been in a battle you do. Now, no mud on my seats. I vacuumed the car right out this morning."

Nat scrambled into the back of the black car. He was so out of breath he could scarcely trust himself to speak.

It wasn't what he had planned. He'd intended to hide in the boot, be driven off when they left and climb out after the car had stopped. It was a mad idea, but it might have worked. He'd never dreamt they had a chauffeur.

"You've to go to Salisbury," Nat blurted out. "Take me to Salisbury."

The chauffeur, a podgy man with a shiny pink forehead and bald head criss-crossed with a few carefully smoothed strands of hair, stared at Nat through watery eyes.

"My! Where've you lost your breath then?" He twisted back in his seat and examined himself in the mirror, patting his pink scalp. "And lost your manners too, if you ask me."

"Please," gasped Nat.

"We've got to wait for your uncle. I'm not driving up through that mud again, ruining my chassis, playing along with your hide-and-seek game. If you were my nephew I wouldn't put up with it."

"Nephew ... ?"

"I suppose you've left your uncle to say goodbye to your friends. I hope you remembered your Ps and Qs. I mean, that's kids isn't it these days, not taught any manners. I blame the parents, I do ..."

"I've thanked them already," Nat tried. The chauffeur didn't know; he'd been told some story. "My uncle is staying for tea – he said my friends will drive him home later."

"Home," chuckled the man. "They're not taking him back to London then?"

"He might stay the night," Nat gabbled, hardly able to sit still on the seat. "I've got to go to Salisbury, to the station – to meet my mum."

"That don't sound right," said the man, rubbing his fleshy neck. "What am I meant to do, sleep in the car?"

"Then we're to bring Mum back for the party, and we'll most likely all go back to London together."

"Well, I don't know, I'm sure. This is a limousine service, this is. I never take more than three passengers, one in the front and two in the back. I mean, I'm not running some come-and-go taxi service. This is class, this is – not family outing hire."

"My uncle told me he'd pay extra..." Nat struggled with his mounting panic.

The man pulled a navy chauffeur's cap across his strands of hair and eased black leather driving gloves over his pudgy hands. "And I'll charge him extra if there's so much as a scratch on my car. Making me park down beside a holly bush, I ask you; said he

101

wanted to surprise you! Bit old to be playing hide and seek, aren't you? At your age I was a Scout, learning my cookery badge ..."

Nat glanced nervously through the back window.

"We'll be late. Mum will be waiting."

The chauffeur smoothed the tight black leather down over each finger in turn.

"And I don't mind telling you, that uncle of yours is an odd customer. The places we've been ... I can't think why he didn't hire a jeep and drive it himself, except he says he's from abroad – not used to British cars and driving on the left. And that sour-faced radio buff with him, never says a word, but sits tuning in to the police radio, never listening to a decent bit of music. He gives me the creeps."

"He's another uncle," said Nat. He glanced at his watch. He'd been in the car a good ten minutes already.

"I thought he was your older brother?"

"Oh ..." muttered Nat desperately. "He's a half-brother, more like an uncle."

The powerful engine roared into action at last as the car backed out from under the trees and turned into the road.

Nat sighed with relief and looked behind him out of the back window. He could still see the white police car and the yellow Volkswagen parked at the top of the track outside the farmhouse. The men in black were nowhere to be seen.

The chauffeur glanced up the track as the car accelerated into the lane. "Quite a party they've got up there now. Well I hope the gentlemen enjoyed the walk," he sniffed dismissively. "Most people, who hire my limousine like to arrive in style, make a good impression. I do it properly, with a bit of class. Open the doors, have an umbrella ready if it's raining ..."

The car purred along, down the village street. Nat sank back into his deep seat as they passed the village shop, before remembering that the car windows were tinted, and no one could see him.

He'd never been in a car like this. It was like a floating lounge – it glided so smoothly, it didn't feel like driving. Nat stretched out his legs and they still didn't reach the seats in front of him.

Nat glanced up and was aware of the chauffeur looking at him in the rear-view mirror. Nat edged over into the corner, pretending to rest his head on the side, to get out of the chauffeur's line of vision.

"Do you know, I've a feeling I've seen you before ... but you're not a bit like your uncle, or your brother. Funny, isn't it, the way you can feel you've met someone before?"

Nat tried to make a polite grunt. He didn't dare speak.

"You know, I sometimes think there's something to this reincarnation business. A year ago I was watching a video with the wife, old cowboy film it was, out in the American West, and there was this group of cowboys, and one looked a bit like me: well-covered, muscular, and I knew – I just knew it was me. That was me in another life. Strange, isn't it?"

Nat grunted again as the car sped up the hill, leaving the village behind.

"What I mean to say is, you've got a spiritual air. Perhaps we've met in another life?"

"Yes, maybe," said Nat.

He couldn't cope with this life, so he certainly hoped there weren't any more lives he had to get through.

He'd get the chauffeur to drop him at Salisbury station. There had to be a bus stop there. He'd get on the first bus and ask for Lower Ebbsbourne. If it was the wrong bus they'd tell him the right one and where to catch it.

It seemed pretty simple now, so long as he could keep the chauffeur off dangerous subjects and no one caught up with them.

"Course, I like the horoscopes. Never start the day without reading Madame Firendo, in the *Daily Standard*. She is truly amazing ... Always gets it right. 'You will meet a trying stranger,' she said today. I reckon that must be you. Mind you keep those muddy shoes off my seats. What's your sign? Here—"

The chauffeur fiddled with a cubbyhole beside his driving seat. Nat had to stop the man looking at the paper, there was sure to be a photo in it.

"I'll read – I'll read it!" he shouted.

"No need to shout in me ear, son," said the chauffeur, but he was smiling. "I can't wait to read mine either in the morning. I never so much as put the key in the ignition until I've read it."

The chauffeur lifted the paper in his black gloved hand and tossed it back over his shoulder.

"Always check it, son. Don't want to miss a useful warning."

Nat's hand shook as he turned the pages.

"Go on – let's hear it."

There was the photograph, on one of the inside pages. Nat was furious with the stupid boy in school uniform staring back at him. How had he got himself into this mess? Nat wondered whether to tear the page out. No, better leave it. The man would only ask him what he was doing.

Nat read the first horoscope he saw. Someone had circled it with a pen.

"A demanding day. You will meet a trying stranger, but a little patience and good humour will help all round. Your reward will come in the evening, with excellent prospects for romance."

"Well I never," cried the man. "Same sign as mine! Romance, eh! When's your birthday, son?"

"February the eighteenth," said Nat unthinkingly.

"February the eighteenth! Don't be daft. That's Aquarius. You've just read Taurus: May, same as me. Why did you read—?"

Something started buzzing.

"Don't tell me you've got it wrong. I mean—"

The buzzing went on. It was coming from between the two deep seats in front of Nat. For the first time Nat saw the telephone, a red light flashing on its receiver.

The chauffeur turned, an important smile on his face as he stretched out his hand, but Nat lunged and snatched up the receiver first.

Chapter Thirteen

THE CAR swerved. Trees came towards the front window, directly in the path of the car. There was a violent bump and the noise of grating and crushing metal. The trees appeared to tilt on their sides and then disappeared from view. The car rolled down a slope and came to rest.

"Mr Douglas, Mr Douglas," went the voice in the phone. "Mr Douglas. Are you there? What has happened? I asked you to wait out of sight ..."

The chauffeur groaned from somewhere to the side of Nat. Nat was tipped sideways, imprisoned in his seatbelt. He had to get out. He must get away before someone found them.

He pressed the catch on his seatbelt and it loosened. The chauffeur groaned again.

"Are you all right?" said Nat.

"No, I am not! What did you think you were doing, you stupid idiot?"

Nat peered round the front seat. The chauffeur lay on his side, white-faced.

"I can't see what's wrong. There's no blood."

The man groaned: "My car, you fool, my beautiful car ... that's what's wrong. What's going to happen to Walter Douglas Limousine Service? Killing me, it is." The man struggled with the catch on his seatbelt. "Can't get this thing off. They said they were the latest: never fail in a crash. I'm going to have to blast myself out of this now."

"I'll get help," said Nat.

He tried his door but it wouldn't open. He slid to the other end of the seat and tried the opposite door. It was locked too.

"The doors are locked."

"Course they are – central locking," groaned the man. "Always drive with them locked. Anyone could jump into the car – specially a limousine like this."

"Unlock them!"

"I can't. The door with the locking catch is crushed," the man sobbed. "Just look at this mess—" He turned his head back, tears in his eyes. "And it's – it's the last time I'm having a bloomin' kid in any car of mine!"

They were trapped. A car would drive round the corner any minute and spot the crashed limousine, toppled as it was half down a ditch. Nat grabbed the first thing he could reach: the phone receiver, and hammered at his window.

"What are you doing?" the chauffeur whimpered.

Nat kept on hammering. Quite suddenly the window cracked into a crazed pattern. Nat picked up his bag and pressed it hard against the cracked glass. The window fell out, almost in one piece, but an alarm started up, shrieking in his ear.

Gingerly, he climbed through the window.

"I'm going for help."

At that moment two women, one iron-haired and towering in a dull green raincoat and the other round and shiny in a yellow mac with matching rainhat, walked round the corner. They were pulled by two dogs, straining on leads. The dogs growled and the women winced at the shrieking alarm. Nat clambered up the bank as the women drew level and stared in amazement at the upturned car.

"My God!" the woman in green exclaimed suddenly.

The stout woman waddled forward, her shiny mac crackling.

"Are you all right, dear? What happened?"

"There's a man – a man in the car," stuttered Nat.

The two women clambered heavily down the bank.

Beside the road Nat saw the red letterbox, toppled on its side. They must have swerved across the road and hit it. One side of the car front was completely crushed.

"Joan," announced the woman in green. "You go and call for help – and you, boy, what's your name? You weren't in the car were you?"

"No – no."

"Thank heavens for that! For a moment I thought you had just got out of the car."

"No."

"Run along home now. There's nothing a child can do here. How very odd! The window's smashed in at the back, the opposite side of the driver, and there's blood on the window sill."

The woman in yellow seemed to be reluctant to leave.

"What about shock, surely the man is in shock? Are you sure you'll be all right on your own, Sylvia dear?"

"Don't dither, Joan. Take the dogs and go."

Nat didn't want to go anywhere with the stout lady. Suddenly he grabbed his bag and ran on down the lane, past the toppled postbox. Dazed and confused, he didn't know where he was going. He saw a line of cottages and a path leading round beside them ... Follow that – get away from the road.

He ran along the path until it opened out on to a football pitch with a playground on one side. It was some sort of recreation ground, empty of children now. They'd all be at school.

The women had been so surprised that they hadn't questioned why he wasn't at school. They'd gabbled on, hardly noticing him.

A stone wall bordered the recreation ground at one side, closing off a grey church with squat grey tower. Nat headed towards the church, clambered over the wall and found himself surrounded by graves. Some

110

had wonky-looking headstones, some were squared off with rusty iron railings and some were moss-covered raised stone tables.

Nat stumbled through until his legs collapsed beneath him. They had been shaking all the time but he hadn't noticed until now. His jeans were sticky too, and hurt.

No – his jeans couldn't hurt. It must be his knee. Yes, his knee was hurting.

Nat slumped against a marble headstone which read '*Hubert Bridge – In Loving Memory of a Dear Father*', and examined his leg. His jeans were split and the torn sides stuck to a narrow cut in a sticky, bloody mess at the top of his knee. He must have cut himself when he squeezed through the car window, and he had never felt a thing.

What was he going to do? It had all happened so fast, he could hardly think. Better not move now – a graveyard was as safe as anywhere.

Nat shivered and stared up at the grey sky. At least the rain had stopped. But he was still cold and bouts of shivering quivered through him as he stared blankly ahead.

Wait a bit. He was down now – on the floor. But he'd work it out when he got his breath.

The whine of an approaching siren woke him roughly from his daze. Was it an ambulance, or a police car, or a truck to tow the smashed car away? The siren crescendoed past the cottages and stopped.

Were they coming for him? He didn't know, his

111

head was in such a muddle. No ... They were going to Mr Douglas, trapped in his car.

Nat felt sick in the pit of his stomach. He couldn't have eaten a thing but he was dying for a drink.

Keep down, don't let anyone see you.

Nat crawled through the graveyard like an ungainly crab, one knee bent, the hurt knee extended so as not to touch the ground. He saw water, dark and stagnant, in vases of dead flowers left on the graves, but he couldn't fancy the water from those. Then, at one side, next to a dump high with rotting leaves and dead flowers, he saw a tap on the end of a long pipe.

He dragged himself over and lay beneath the spout. The water splashed freezing cold on to his face and hair, odd dribbles trickling into the corners of his mouth.

It tasted delicious. Nat had never believed water could taste so good.

Then he sat up, pulled his spare T-shirt out of his kit bag, moistened the sleeve and dabbed at his gaping jeans. The cut was to one side of the knee. It had stopped bleeding but he knew he should wash the dirt out. He carefully probed out the dirt, thinking of Mum. Then he splashed it with water, as Mum had done to his grazes when he was little.

What would she be doing now, thinking now?

Suddenly Nat felt very alone. But he was always alone really, he'd got used to that. When he was with Gemma or Adam and Sean the loneliness faded a little, as it had when he had helped that ridiculous kid in the barn look after the sick lamb; or when he and Mum sat

112

in front of the telly, their tea on their knees, and watched a funny programme together, roaring with laughter. Then, for a little while, he wasn't lonely.

But if people didn't much take to you, you had to give up minding about loneliness. It was something you got used to.

"I don't want to be in goal. I'm always in goal."

"You're a good goalie, James. Anyway, you can't run very fast."

"I can! I just don't ever get the chance. And it's cold hanging round goal."

The voices were the other side of the graveyard wall, coming from the recreation ground.

Nat sat up suddenly. He'd been lolling for ages, remembering, pondering. Feeling sorry for himself, that's what he'd been doing. Well, that wouldn't get him anywhere!

The voices came from a group of boys running on to the pitch. School must be over.

Nat was alert to the voices. He wanted to watch the boys, see them play, immerse himself in a normal world again.

"Why didn't you bring your good ball?"

"I'm keeping that to play with my dad at the weekend."

"This one's a dud. It's got a puncture."

"It hasn't."

"I know a slow puncture – and this is a slow puncture."

"Give it back then. We won't play."

"Come on, you two. Stop arguing! We're getting cold. We can manage with Andrew's ball."

The boys threw their jackets to the ground and ran on to the pitch.

At Nat's school the playground was tarmacked. The playing fields the school shared with other schools were a good few miles away. There was nowhere to play football in the evenings, except round the flats, and then ball games were supposed to be forbidden. These kids didn't know how lucky they were. A whole recreation ground of their own!

"What's that boy doing in there?"

A girl with dark, straggly hair sauntered past, arm in arm with a friend. She peered over the wall and pointed at Nat.

"It's a spook, a ghost," giggled the second girl, round as a balloon in a puffy pink jacket.

What a cheek! Nat sank down behind the wall, trying to look his usual scornful self. The girls came and stood the other side of the wall.

"Eek!" screeched the first girl above Nat's head. "A ghost – in the graveyard! Did you see how white he was, Emma, all sickly and rotting?"

Emma giggled. "He's disappeared all right now."

"He's a frightened ghost," said the first girl. "A cowardly, whimpish ghost that ain't used to brave girls like us."

Nat jumped up angrily. All the tension the car crash had built up was itching to burst out and descend with fury on the girls. Nobody talked to him like that and got away with it. He'd give them a good fright, stop their cheek.

No! He had to calm down, control himself. He couldn't risk attracting attention to himself.

Nat gripped his hands at his sides, picked up his bag and walked, casually, up the path to the church door.

He'd walked away. He'd never have done it before.

The anger still pounded in his ears, but a sense of triumph came over him. He hadn't blown it. He was in control again and off the floor.

Then he remembered, Madame Firendo: "Excellent prospects for romance." He could do without that one for sure.

The iron handle on the heavy wooden door creaked as Nat turned it. The door groaned open, revealing a dark interior. The chill air seemed to rush at Nat, full of musty smells. The church was like an eerie cavern, even darker than the grey afternoon outside, apart from a faint light that struggled through the stained-glass windows.

Nat stared at the stone tombs and their out-stretched, life-size figures; at the massive wooden crucifix hanging on the wall; at the empty dark pews, with their prayerbooks lined up for invisible readers. It was like a creepy museum, full of dead people. A dank, musty-smelling museum.

But it had to be a good place to hide.

There was a door in the back wall of the church. He'd try that. He'd feel more comfortable somewhere smaller.

He walked to the back of the church, his trainers padding on the cold stones and the church so quiet he could hear his own breathing.

The door led to a room full of shapeless clothes. Along one wall were rows of pegs with long blue shirts, together with what looked like a load of white table-cloths.

Nat shivered. It was cold in here too. He pushed his bag under the bench beneath the row of shirts and sat down, hugging his knees to his chest.

But the cold didn't get any better. He pulled the thick envelope out of his bag and shoved it under his sweater, tucking it into the waistband of his jeans. A down and out who slept in the market at home always stuffed his clothes with newspaper to keep warm. He didn't dare get his sleeping bag out. What if he had to run for it, or worse, fell asleep?

One of those shirts would do – an extra layer.

Nat unhooked a blue shirt. It wasn't big enough to wrap round him like a blanket, so he slipped it over his head. It was voluminous and loose, completely covering his sweater, and it was so long it trailed to the floor at his feet. He curled up on the bench. If he got any colder he could always put another shirt on top.

He might as well hide there until the rescue services and Mr Douglas were well out of the way. He'd get away in the dark, find the road to Salisbury and walk through the night.

But he had to move fast. It was Friday already, the congress started tomorrow and he hadn't come this far to miss Professor Keeping.

Chapter Fourteen

IT WAS pitch dark when Nat decided to move. He didn't want to go out through the church again. What if he had to feel his way past those horrible tombs?

Nat was pulling his bag from under the bench when a grating sound of metal cut through the silence. The handle of the church door was being turned. Then came the slow groan of the door swinging open.

Nat leapt up and tried to pull himself back into the line of blue shirts hanging on the wall. Slow but purposeful footsteps rang out across the stone floor.

Who was it? They seemed to know where they were going. The steps grew closer and louder, and then stopped at the door to Nat's room.

A blinding light suddenly illuminated the white walls and line of blue shirts. Nat blinked. An old man in a dark suit was striding through the door towards Nat, both hands outstretched in front of him.

Nat was on his feet, tripping in his long blue shirt,

ready to fight him off, but the man stopped a mere metre from him.

"Welcome!" he said, smiling broadly, in an unexpectedly loud, deep voice. He had a pale wrinkled face and tiny blue eyes, bright as beads, twinkling beneath bushy white eyebrows. The matching bushy ring of white hair trembled as: "Welcome, dear boy!" he announced again.

Nat couldn't avoid the insistent smile and the penetrating blue eyes. One half of him told him to look away, while the other half wanted to return the smile.

"I was hoping you would come. You can't imagine how delighted I am. You're a big boy, though. Your voice hasn't broken, I hope?"

Nat shook his head in amazement.

"You are special. God has sent you to us."

Nat kept his mouth shut. He wasn't sure how much this old man knew, or God knew for that matter.

"And you've found a gown, I see – excellent!"

Nat looked down in surprise at his trailing blue shirt.

"They're new," said the old man, white hair trembling, smiling with delight. "Just arrived ..."

The outer door of the church groaned again and giggling voices burst in, growing shriller as they approached. The door opened and four or five girls ambled in, stopped, and stared at Nat.

One girl tossed her straggly dark hair back from her face, so as to whisper behind her hand: "No! The ghost!"

119

It was so loud, Nat heard. She had meant them all to hear.

A girl who looked like a plump strawberry whip giggled madly. Then the other girls started giggling, as if on cue.

Nat recognised Emma, the girl in the pink jacket, and her cheeky friend: they were the girls from the recreation ground.

"Now, um ... er ... your name, dear boy?" said the old man.

"John ... Jones," said Nat quickly.

"John Jones? My memory is getting so bad. Didn't you come to my Sunday school when you were a little boy?"

"I don't know him. Where's he from?" said the girl with straggly hair insistently. "He's not at our school."

"My dear Linda, our new member is not a 'him', but John, and just because we have had no boys in the choir for so long is no reason not to offer him the heartiest of welcomes."

Linda sniffed and turned to whisper to her friend.

"Well, John," smiled the white-haired man, "you and I are the only males in the choir, but I have only just started advertising for boys and men in the village, and I am delighted to have my first recruit so quickly."

Linda, behind the old man, stuck out her tongue at Nat. For the second time that day, Nat longed to give her a shock she wouldn't forget.

"Such is the temptation of the new recreation ground, that we seem to have lost all our boys to the

120

village football team," the vicar smiled weakly. "An excellent under-thirteen team, I hear."

"What's wrong with choirgirls then, vicar?" demanded the pink strawberry whip of a girl.

"My dear, absolutely nothing. Very fine singers and I'm most grateful," beamed the vicar. "But I want balance in the choir. I want boys and men too."

At this the door opened and in came three ladies, none of them young. To Nat's dismay he recognised the crackling shiny mac of the fat lady at the postbox earlier.

"Good evening, Mrs Protheroe and Miss Sims and Mrs Pilkington-Wingate!"

One woman smiled shyly, another nodded her head with a curt smile, while the fat lady just stared at Nat.

"But that boy ... This afternoon ... I saw him ... "

"I don't think we should overwhelm John Jones with questions, Mrs Protheroe. Let us welcome him instead."

She turned to the line of pegs and hung up her yellow mac. Fortunately she seemed more interested in the new blue shirts than in Nat. Her face was soon smothered in blue cloth as she struggled to pull the shirt down over a figure that curved in and out in wavy bumps, like the old mattress on Mum's bed. She emerged red-faced and seemed to forget all about Nat.

Nat shook himself. What was going on, and how could he get away from all these women?

He couldn't be more obvious than the only boy

121

among a crowd of women and girls. But if he ran off now, suddenly, he'd draw attention to himself, so it might make sense to wait and just leave at the end. If anyone had any idea where he had been hiding, they wouldn't be able to touch him if he left in a crowd. Then he should easily be able to slip away from the group in the dark.

The vicar approached Nat with a silver cross on a long wooden stick.

"... a little practice of processing in our new gowns. We don't want any tripping over on Sunday, do we?" And he chuckled, smiling round at the admiring circle of women. "John, as our newest member, I would like you to do the honours and carry the cross."

He couldn't get out of it. Reluctantly Nat took the heavy cross. He heard a giggle behind him, and he had to restrain himself from using the cross to give a good poke at the gaggle of girls chattering behind. What on earth would Adam and Sean think of him? He'd have to keep quiet about this.

"Set a steady, dignified pace, John. Miss Sims – start the organ!"

There was a blast of discordant sound from the organ. The vicar closed his blue eyes for a moment, then opened them and smiled encouragingly at Nat.

It was hopeless. Miss Sims sometimes played fast, and sometimes, when she came to a difficult bit, slowed down almost to a stop.

Somehow Nat got to the top of the church, up the steps towards the altar, with the girls whispering behind him.

"Well done, dear boy." The low voice of the vicar was close to his ear. "A splendid start."

Nat glanced up into the smiling blue eyes. For some stupid reason he felt pleased with himself. Miss Sims played atrociously, with no regular beat to her playing, but the vicar obviously thought Nat had done a good enough job.

They started with 'Praise, my soul, the King of heaven', which Miss Sims seemed to know, as she played it much too fast. Nat sort of knew it too, because Mum often irritated him singing along to *Songs of Praise* on telly, and he'd heard her singing it in the kitchen too.

"A fine voice, excellent tone!" The vicar was bending over Nat's ear again.

Nat could feel himself reddening with pleasure. He was surprised the vicar had noticed, as the old man himself had a bellow that drowned all neighbouring sounds. "Sing out! You mustn't keep a good voice hidden."

Nat did like singing, the vicar was right. Not that he had much chance, except in the bath.

Then they started on a chorus, really modern, like a pop song, with a cheery, swinging tune. Miss Sims was in a lot of trouble on the organ, so the vicar beat time, hammering with his hymn book on the pew.

123

"Alleluia! Alleluia!
The good Lord loves us all,
Alleluia! Alleluia! ..."

Nat was belting it out. It felt good to loosen his guard, stop holding himself in so tight, let off steam and shout it out. "Alleluia! Alle—"

It took him a few moments to register the two men in dark overcoats who were sidling round the pews at the side of the church.

"The church is closed, gentlemen, for choir practice," called out the vicar as Miss Sims crashed the last notes on the lilting chorus. "Can you come back tomorrow? We are open all day for prayer and meditation."

But the men kept on walking, up the nave, up the steps to the choir stalls.

The older of the two, dressed in a black coat as if he was going to a funeral, removed his black hat and held it against his chest. Then he raised his face, wreathed in a sickly smile, but one dark eye was hard and unsmiling. The other, half hidden by a drooping lid, appeared to wink.

Despite the cold church, Nat was overcome with a hot stickiness, trapped by the enveloping blue shirt.

"We are looking, sir ... I wonder if you could help ..." came a respectful, almost whining voice.

"You've come for the choir," exclaimed the vicar. "How absolutely splendid! You've just made it for the last half-hour. Plenty of room behind young John here."

The men looked at one another and then at Nat. Then the older man made a motion forward with his hand and the younger man, tall and thin, followed behind.

Nat felt as if he had been at the top of a spiral, head in the clouds, and now, like a tornado, he was whizzing round in circles, crashing to the ground. He kept his eyes glued to his hymn book.

The two men edged past, into place behind him. Nat could hear their laboured breathing. They must have been in a hurry, getting to the church.

"We will try hymn number fifty-seven: 'God works in wondrous ways'," announced the vicar above Nat's ear. "Indeed, how true – how true! Miss Sims, throw yourself into this, dear lady. Pull the organ stops out, and let us thrill to the music."

Women's voices trilled out, girls swayed in time as they sang, the vicar belted the words out fit to burst, while from behind Nat came a faint, half-hearted growling.

The vicar held up his hand after the first two verses, and turned to the men beside him. Nat heard his loud, confidential whisper: "Gentlemen, the tune is printed in the hymn book. If you follow the tune you can't go wrong," then, more loudly, closer to Nat, "and, John, more of that magnificent voice. It seems to have quite disappeared!"

"I need – need the toilet," whispered Nat urgently.

"The toilet, did you say?" Opposite there was a snigger from the straggly-haired girl and a giggle from the strawberry whip. "Dear me! We don't have a lavatory in church. You'll have to go out and into the vicarage and tell my wife."

Nat was already halfway out of his pew.

"Don't dawdle. No stopping for football on the recreation ground!" The vicar's laughter at his own joke echoed behind Nat as he set off rapidly down the aisle. Then, more faintly, "No, sir, John is very able to seek out the way alone; he used to attend my Sunday school in the vicarage. We can't disrupt the practice further, and a little dark won't hurt him: we are all in God's keeping."

The heavy wooden door creaked shut behind Nat. He hadn't dared arouse suspicion by collecting his kit bag from the room at the back, but at least he had Dr Buxton's envelope. He could feel the sharp corners digging into his chest.

As soon as the choir practice was over he knew the two men would be after him. He knew for sure now that they were determined to get him. And if they had beaten up the little girl with her chubby little face and tangled gold curls, they wouldn't hesitate, in any way they could, to hurt him to keep him quiet.

He'd let his guard slip with all that singing – got carried away.

He should have learnt by now that when things looked as if they might be going all right, they usually took a nose dive. He'd been caught off guard, laid himself open to a smashing right hook.

The darkness was dense and suffocating. It took him some time to focus his eyes, until he could just make out the pale thread of the stone path. He hitched up his long shirt in his hands and hurried down the path.

Outside the gate he hesitated. Which way to go?

He stepped back, scraping his hand on – a bicycle leaning against the graveyard wall. His hands eagerly explored the old-fashioned heavy bike, a woman's bike with a wicker basket on the front.

Nat struggled out of the long shirt and tried to stuff it into the basket. He had to pull out a bit of plastic to make room for it. Buttons – there were buttons on the plastic. It was some sort of rain cape.

He buttoned it round his shoulders, pulling the drawstring tight on the hood so that most of his face was covered, then he pushed on the pedals, wobbled up on to the seat, and slammed his feet down and forward, pedalling with every muscle in his legs straining.

He hadn't a clue where he was heading, and he didn't care. It was enough to get away.

Chapter Fifteen

NAT FORCED the stiff pedals round and round. It was a tank of a bike with not a gear in sight. Whoever usually rode it must go at a snail's pace. The old-fashioned seat forced him to sit upright, but as he passed each dim streetlight, he tried to lower his face.

A car was approaching from behind. Nat heard the idling sound as the car slowed down, quite close now. Surely they hadn't got out of the church already ...

"Lights, Miss Sims! You haven't got your lights on," called a man from the car window.

Nat wobbled and nearly fell off the bike with fright. He hadn't noticed; the streetlights had been bright enough. A square torch was clipped to the handlebars. He twiddled the nob on top and a beam of weak yellow light quivered into the dark ahead.

The car hooted twice and drove slowly past. Nat had the impression of a smiling face and the wave of a pale hand, before it was swallowed up by the darkness.

He took a deep breath. That had been too close for comfort! Good thing he had worn the cape.

The lampposts came to an end at the edge of the village and the road forked. Either branch led into blinding darkness.

Nat stopped beneath a signpost. He narrowed his eyes but he couldn't make out the letters in the dim light. Hauling the bike up, he tried to point the wavering torch at the sign, but he couldn't hold the heavy bike steady. Then he heard the distant roar. A car was accelerating at speed somewhere behind him. Nat leapt on to the bike.

Which way to take? The smaller one – to the right. He pedalled a few metres and then jumped off, pulling the bike into an opening in a field.

The car roared to the junction and braked with a screech. Nat could see the flood of powerful headlights lighting up the white sign, and then the car accelerated along the other road, to the left.

Nat stood holding the bike to him, rigid with fear, chilled by the clammy sweat trickling down his back.

In the distance he heard the car's drone growing fainter and fainter, until his straining ears lost it altogether. Shakily he climbed back on the bike and cycled on.

The lane meandered on into rough track, track that was gritty and rutted. It was difficult making much headway, but he had to keep going. His legs were shaking and exhausted; push on – he'd never let them catch him now.

Nat was used to yellow-tinged city night, not this utter blackness. He couldn't see a single star. A faint paling of charcoal cloud covered the moon.

At times the bike ran up on grass when he missed the track. There were no hedges; he must be in some sort of open country, like a moor. Stones rattled and shook the bike frame, forcing him to stand to pedal.

He'd be quicker on foot. He hid the bike behind a bush with sharp thorns and ran on, until he realised he was running on smooth wet grass.

Had he lost the track or had it run out?

He didn't know, but he had to keep going. Rough stalks, scratchy bushes, prickly leaves, he kicked his way through until his foot slid on wet grass, sinking down into cold water and mud.

Grabbing wildly at a branch, Nat pulled his leg back. It came out of the mud with a squelching, sucking sound. Marsh ... he must be on boggy ground.

It was too dangerous going on in the dark, blundering through sinking mud. He might as well stop and hide for the night.

Nat moved back to higher, firmer ground, bumping into a massive tree. The grass beneath was sodden, so he crouched with his back to the trunk.

He was so cold and exhausted.

He couldn't see a thing. The blackness was like a smothering blanket. If only it was a blanket! He shivered and hugged himself and thought longingly of his sleeping bag in the church.

Would it be warm at Mr Prendergast's prison

school in the country? It had to be better than this – warm beds, hot baths, baking food.

What was the point of going on? He must be so near Salisbury, but as he got closer it seemed harder and harder to make it. He could go back to that vicar; he had been so pleased to see Nat, tell him all about it.

Hold on! Hadn't he lied to the vicar with the choirboy pretence? Why would the vicar believe him now?

"You're on your own," he muttered grimly to himself, rocking on his heels. "Nobody gives a damn about what really happened, so get wise to it!"

Lie at their feet, knocked down and hear them start to count.

No! He could still fight – morning had to come.

Sometimes he dozed and woke with aching back and cold, numb legs. Another time he stood up, grabbed the tree trunk with one hand and ran and ran, circling the tree until he was panting and almost warm. But the cold soon crept back.

The night sounds were strange, like in an alien world: little rustlings, the wind moaning in overhead branches, a screaming call in the night sky, and a hoarse barking in the bushes behind.

Used to being alone ... Pretend the noises were the telly ...

But he knew he had no choice. He drifted back to sleep, a sleep that ached with wet and cold and visions of tombs in a dark church, with stone men in black hats and coats stretched out on marble tomb tops.

A stone figure was climbing down off the tomb and coming towards him. Nat backed away but he was caught up against the wall. The man had a grey, expressionless face. He was stretching out a hand.

Nat wriggled, but he couldn't escape the insistent cold grip.

"No!" he screamed. "Get your hands off me!"

"Come on, lad. What do you think I am: some pervert?" whispered a voice insistently beside him.

Nat opened one eye to stare into a grey soup. Set in the soup were the darker shadows of faces, insubstantial faces, here and there a dark eyebrow taut with disapproval. A bony face, big ears sticking out beneath an ancient hat, drew close to Nat's face. A long finger was held up to thin, pursed lips.

"Shh!" the lips mouthed.

Nat tried to shake off the hand on his arm and stagger to his feet. His legs were so stiff and numb he toppled and fell against the warm, bony body hung about with an enormous jacket.

"Absolutely essential we amend the rules, keep children away," mouthed the stiff moustache of another disembodied grey face. "Look at the boy: not properly equipped, dreadful shiny red cape – bloody nuisance, children!"

"Looks half dead, if you ask me," came a disapproving woman's voice, and yet another grey face peered through the soup.

"What—" Nat began.

"Someone keep him quiet, or he'll ruin it."

Nat stared around him, dazed, trying to remember where he was. Was he in the church? No – he dreamt that. He had cycled on to some rough ground, hadn't he, with a tree?

"Leave him to me," whispered the bony face. "I'll get my flask and give him a drop of tea. He's cold enough to sink the *Titanic*."

"Stanley," said the irritated female voice, "you're much too good! I wouldn't have bothered, myself. We haven't come all this way to baby sit."

Nat was propped against the tree. His hands hurt; the man was rubbing them. Then a plastic beaker, the heat of its contents bathing Nat's face with steam, was shoved between his lips. Nothing in all Nat's life had ever tasted so good: hot, sweet tea, smelling of plastic, poured into his mouth.

"Won't have long to wait now. You got here early!"

Nat grunted. The man seemed quite happy with that as an explanation.

"Dawn's breaking now. Nice ground mist. Just what we need as cover."

Nat nodded. The grey soup – of course, it was mist. As the dark lightened, the mist was becoming whiter.

"Thanks," said Nat as he grabbed the beaker with both hands now.

"I was your sort of age when I got on to this game. Did some crazy things too, till I knew what I was up to!"

133

Suddenly, from all around, a tide of murmurs fluttered up. The man set down the thermos flask, sprang to his feet and raised something black and shiny to his face.

Nat staggered to his feet. His caution had returned with the feeling in his legs. Everywhere, poking through the white mist, were heads, some with woolly green hats on, some with army-style camouflage caps, some with wet, shining hair in shades of straw, brown and grey, while to each disembodied head was held a pair of binoculars.

"A goshawk!" came an excited woman's whisper. "Has someone told Stanley? He's stuck with that wretched boy."

"It's OK, I saw it," the thin lips above Nat whispered.

"It was after that pied flycatcher for its breakfast – d'ya see it?" came the hoarser whisper of the grey moustache.

"Pied flycatcher, was it? Shush – listen!" whispered Stanley.

Nat could hear dripping from the branches above him. The rustlings of the night were gone, but here and there a bird called.

"Dawn," murmured Stanley, his bony face dropping down again beside Nat. "There's no magic like the dawn chorus in spring."

"Mmnm," said Nat. He was beginning to come to. He was with a crowd of lunatics, but they had to have come from somewhere. If he was careful, he might be able to get a lift out of this place, and if the mist held, they might never recognise him.

The tide of murmurs welled up again.

"It's over there!"

A huge speckled bird with stubby brown wings and a long tail glided in and out of the mist overhead and then disappeared.

The mist was thinning now. The chatter around was full of excitement as plastic sandwich boxes emerged from backpacks.

"I don't mind if I don't see another hawk all year," said the woman, her face now visible, under a green fluffy hat.

"From the Continent, I expect," said Stanley. "Come to breed in a nice bit of English damp." He rubbed his hands and bounced from foot to foot: "Goshawk! What a start to the spring season!"

Nat watched him suspiciously. What was wrong with the man? He reminded Nat of a little kid at recess. They got so excited in some game that they never stopped jiggling about and rushing around. As you got older, you learnt to walk more slowly, casual-like.

"And how long have you been twitching, lad?" Stanley's bony face beamed with a row of misshapen teeth as he offered Nat a crumbly biscuit. "Not long, I expect," he said, answering his own question. "Don't tell me you didn't even bring breakfast."

"Twitching?"

"Birdwatching! We're the Salisbury Twitchers. Where are you from then?"

Salisbury! Did the man live in Salisbury? Nat was dying to ask him.

"I live in the city," he mumbled. He didn't feel happy with the questions. "No birds there, just pigeons."

"No birds in the city! The place is full of 'em. You get a great dawn chorus from April to June, round five and six o'clock. We've been twitching in the centre of Salisbury before now, round the cathedral."

Salisbury!

"You don't need to come out here to twitch. You can sleep warm in your own bed in town and still be up to watch the birds at dawn. You got binoculars?"

"No."

"Ask Father Christmas for binoculars. Get a decent pair, mind, no second-rate junk."

It was impossible to stop the man. He was like a can of cola that had been shaken and opened.

"Get yourself a bird list. You'll tick off starlings, sparrows and swifts under roof tiles, even an old shed with a hole in will do for blackbirds and robins. And the owls I've heard at night in town! It was a sick owl I found at your age, got me started on twitching." He held out another biscuit. "Now what are you doing here alone, chasing a goshawk?"

"I live in a flat," gabbled Nat, desperate to stay off awkward questions, but he bit into the delicious sugary butter taste.

"I've got a lady friend lives in a town flat," said Stanley, tipping the thermos flask to extract the last drop of tea. "She's got a feeding shelf on her window-sill, and water holders stuck to the window with rubber suckers. You don't need to freeze in the forest, lad, when you haven't started with your own home ..."

Stanley crushed the empty biscuit pack, screwed the plastic cup back on top of the thermos, and packed them carefully in his old army knapsack.

The man wasn't a lunatic. He was interesting and shared his breakfast. Nat wanted to stay and listen and ask about the screeching bird on the allotment.

"Nasty cut, you've got there. Made a mess of your jeans. Your mother won't be too pleased."

Nat froze. Mum seemed light years away now.

In his mind he could see her, opening his door, staring at his empty bed with her frightened, gerbil eyes.

He had to get back, she would be in a terrible state.

The envelope! He must have lost weight in the last couple of days: his waist band hadn't felt tight with the envelope stuck in. He felt under his sweater. The corners were crushed and bent over and he could feel a crease across the middle. The brown paper had lost its shiny stiffness. It was damp and soft, and a hole in the side exposed papers inside to Nat's searching fingers.

Dr Buxton's papers were safe. But he had to get moving. The men in the church might have found the bike, be on his track.

The sweet biscuit taste rose to his mouth. He felt sick. There was no going back now. He had to get on, deliver the envelope to this Professor Keeping and find out who the men were who were after Dr Buxton's paper, men ruthless enough to silence a little girl who was their only witness.

"... does she know you're here?"

Nat shivered as he stared up blankly at the kind face. In the paling light Nat could make out the unshaven dark bristle edging the jutting jaw.

"Salisbury," Nat struggled. He hadn't heard what the man had been saying. "Salisbury. Mum's there. Could you give me a lift?"

"I'll be happy to," beamed the man. "You go straight home and I won't tell on you. I've got to get back to go to work so—"

A shout went up. The man dropped his army bag to the ground, grabbed his binoculars with one hand and camera with the other.

"Over in the holly copse," whispered a voice urgently. "Eating berries ..."

"Come on, lad," said the bony man. "You wait till you tell your twitching friends in town you've seen a goshawk—"

"I've got to get to Salisbury," began Nat.

"I'm not going until this bird goes," declared the man with surprising firmness. "Richard Law might be going back sooner. He has to get to work early. Which part of Salisbury do you want?"

"Lower Ebbsbourne," said Nat quickly. He'd looked at the envelope so often, the address was engraved in his memory.

"Lower Ebbsbourne!" exploded the man. "That's ten miles or more from Salisbury." He looked back intently at Nat. "It's a good drive from here too. Strange though, because if you walk it as the crow flies, it should be just over that hill somewhere. You could walk it easy. We'll talk about it when I've got a shot of this bird ..." He looked back as if torn as to whether he should stay and question Nat more; then he glanced towards the holly thicket, his face lighting up with excitement, and he was off, disappearing into the white mist.

Nat took off the shiny cape, rolled it up tight under his arm and staggered on stiff legs until he was running uphill.

Chapter Sixteen

OVER THE hill, Stanley had said, straight ahead as the crow flies.

Nat had taken an instant decision. He didn't want to go: he would have given anything to stay and hear what Stanley had to say about the dawn birds, and to find out what he and the other twitchers were up to.

This Professor Keeping – a name, nothing more. Stanley was real and alive.

Nat had once found a pigeon on the road, unable to fly. Mum had said it must have been hit by a car. He'd given it a bit of milk and bread and kept it in a cardboard box in his room, but it was dead by the morning. Mum told him to put it in the dustbin, but he couldn't, so he'd sneaked Mr Birt's spade and buried it behind the shed on the allotment. He hadn't told the gang.

And now ... he hadn't even had a chance to ask Stanley about the screeching bird on the allotment at night.

Nat listened with new ears as he climbed the hill. It was a crazy din, erupting from every tree and bush, of trilling, chirruping and warbling.

He wished he could stop and look for the birds, but he had to get away ... And Stanley said there were birds in town, too. Nat had never heard them; you'd never have caught him awake at five or six in the morning.

The mist had lifted now, except in the lower hollows at the foot of the hill, chased away by the morning sun. Stretching out beneath Nat, from the hill to the horizon, was the most beautiful countryside he had ever seen.

There wasn't a road in sight. Here and there he could make out a farm track, and a glittering stream wandering through boggy grassland, rounding tufts of dark bushes and disappearing into a small wood that clung like an abandoned spider's web to the green hillside opposite.

Nat started as a twig cracked in the bushes in front of him. He pulled in behind a tree as two deer stepped daintily out on slender legs in front of him. He could almost have touched their fawn coats with the white, speckled splodges, but one of them lifted its twitching nose in the air, turned towards Nat and then leapt away, in high bounds, as light as air.

He could stay here for ever, never go back, settle in this wonderful place.

Below him he heard a shout. The twitchers were moving off. Would Stanley wonder about him or assume he'd found a lift?

No, of course he couldn't stay here! He had no clothes, no sleeping bag, no food.

Straight ahead as the crow flies, Stanley had said. But which direction over the hill was straight ahead? He was no longer sure what direction he'd come from, and the twitchers had all disappeared.

He had started uphill again, when he heard a rhythmic thudding. A brown horse was pounding towards him, the rider bent low over the horse's neck. Nat turned to look for somewhere to hide.

A shout! It was no use running away as the rider was already waving and yelling, slowing the horse to walking pace up the hill towards him.

The rider was a girl in an enormous speckled sweater and hard black hat, wearing patched muddy jeans tucked into splattered black boots.

"Oh, I'm sorry," she shouted and then laughed as she came near. "I thought you were someone else." Her face was beaming and shiny beneath the black brim.

The horse lifted its front legs, stepping up towards Nat. He could see the girl clearly now, red-brown curls escaping from the hat, freckled face flushed from the wind and the cold.

"I don't bump into many people out as early as this," she grinned down at Nat. "Only Duncan Elliot: he exercises his pony early too." Then she laughed again, as if at some silly joke. "For a moment I thought ... Well, I thought you were Duncan and something had happened."

Nat stared at her. He'd never seen such green eyes: they were like the new leaves budding on the bushes around, but deeper, more like a green sea. He couldn't think what to say.

"I mean ... I saw something leaping in the air and I thought you'd come off, and I came to see if you were all right."

The girl's grin faded. The freckles on her forehead were drawn together in a worried look as she bent down over her saddle. The green of her eyes seemed to deepen.

"You are all right, are you?"

"It was a deer."

"Sorry! Stupid of me – I didn't bother with my glasses this morning."

The girl's cheeks were flushed a brighter pink with embarrassment at her mistake. She sat upright holding the reins with yellow gloves.

For a moment Nat wouldn't have minded being Duncan Elliot. He stared at the long black boots level with his face. They were well worn and splattered with mud, but beneath the mud they shone with polish.

"You're not one of those birdwatchers, careering around in the valley, are you?" The girl smiled quickly at Nat, as if unsure how to go on with the conversation.

"No," said Nat.

As soon as he'd said it he knew he should have said yes – to stop the questions – but the girl had put him off his guard. He edged back uphill until he was level

143

with the horse's ears, and with the seated girl. He didn't like being talked down to.

The horse stretched out a velvet nose into Nat's jumper, gently nibbling with huge teeth. It snorted and Nat jumped back, laughing, beside himself.

"He's found the biscuit crumbs on my sweater."

The girl pulled the horse's head back with her reins.

"Don't be so greedy, Conker!" she exclaimed. "He thinks of nothing but eating. You wouldn't believe he's already had a breakfast of oats, would you."

Nat stretched out his hand to stroke the warm, soft nose. The horse pulled back its lip revealing long yellow teeth as he snuffled round Nat's sweater again.

"You don't live round here, do you?" said the girl, leaning down to pat the horse's neck.

Nat pulled back his hand. What was the point of pretending? The girl probably knew everyone around here.

"No."

"You're not lost, are you?" she said anxiously. "You must have a map or compass or something."

Nat shrugged.

"You didn't come into the New Forest without a compass or even a map! Do you know where to go? You can get lost for hours here, going round and round in circles. The forest is huge. It goes on for ever, down to the coast even."

The girl chatted quickly, her face changing constantly with little smiles and frowns. You'd always be able to guess what was in her mind, Nat thought. She was as transparent as water fresh from the tap.

"Do you want me to look? I've always got a map with me. Dad wouldn't let me out without a map and compass. I know all around here but if it got foggy I'd be lost in an instant – probably end up in some bog – and Conker could break a leg or something."

She swung her leg over the saddle and landed softly beside Nat on the grass.

She was smaller than him, a slight, neatly made girl.

Nat watched her as she undid a leather wallet at the back of Conker's saddle. Together they crouched over the map on the ground. It wasn't a road map, but a contour map showing hills and marshland, and woods and tracks.

"Now," she looked up, the green eyes smiling, "show me where you're making for?"

Nat frowned. "Lower Ebbsbourne."

"That's a couple of miles away at least," said the girl. "Off the map. But if you follow this path up the hill, along the ridge and through the wood at the top, keeping straight on all the way, you'll come to this track to the left," the girl lifted her finger off the map and began to fold it. "Then follow the track down into the valley the other side and you'll see Lower Ebbsbourne – at least what there is of it. There's only a big old house. They've turned it into a hotel or something. There are a couple of farmhouses near it, only they're not farms any longer, but holiday homes ..."

Lower Ebbsbourne, that was it! So close now.

He liked hearing the girl talk, being with someone his own age again. She was still burbling on. He'd never met such a chatty girl; Gemma said just as little as she needed to keep Nat in his place.

But he had to wake up, get away. Saturday – yes, it must be Saturday. The conference started today.

The girl's voice had faded away. She seemed to have become aware Nat wasn't responding to her chatter.

"Oh, I expect it all looks a bit scary, if you're not used to the forest," she smiled shyly. "If you want, you can come up behind me on Conker and come home for breakfast. I'm sure Dad could help you ... But I'll have to change. I'm going into Salisbury with Mummy to shop."

So she thought he was scared going on alone! If she knew what he'd come through ...

"What do you mean, scared?" he said with the most scathing voice he could muster.

The girl started and blushed. "I didn't mean—"

"And I know what I'm doing and where I'm going," Nat hadn't known before, but he knew now he'd seen the map.

"I thought ... I was only ..." She turned to stuff the map in the saddlebag.

"I'll borrow that, if you don't mind," said Nat in the surly tone he knew so well, but which somehow surprised him. He reached up and grabbed the map.

"No ... Well, yes ... I suppose it's all right. It's Dad's. I should really clear it with him first, but if I say you were lost ... I mean not that you are ... I'm sure he

146

won't mind." The girl looked confused and hurt. "Could – could you send it back then, when you've finished with it? To Jenny Livingstone, at Boveridge Farm. You won't forget it because the farm is down on the right-hand corner, the only one on the map ... Please."

Nat grunted.

The girl with her elastic-band smile, her black leather boots and her stupid horse – he could just see her having breakfast with her father at their farm. He hated her. He hated her for living where she did, for her beaming face and helpful father ... so ... so she could keep him!

The girl stood up and faced him. The green eyes flashed with anger but for once her mouth was shut, tight shut.

"You might say thank you," she burst out, blinking quickly.

She spun round and stretched a foot up to the stirrup. The pony edged down the slope, frightened by the angry voices. The slope was too steep for her to mount. She tried a second time but couldn't pull herself up the height of the slope.

"Conker's nervous. Could you please give me a leg up? Push up my other leg."

The anger drained out of Nat as suddenly as it had come.

He wanted her to stay, to chat to him again and smile. He pushed the muddy boot up, his face close to hers.

Suddenly she froze in horror.

"I know who you are," she whispered. "I've seen you before." Her voice rose in panic. "Let go of my leg!"

But she was only halfway over. Nat held on to her, shoving until she was in the saddle. Then he let go and wiped his muddy hands on his jeans.

She stared down at Nat in horror, as if her green eyes didn't dare leave his face, then gathered the reins in her yellow gloves and turned Conker round.

"You're ... you're ..."

"I'm not!" cried Nat desperately.

She broke into a trot, then a canter down the hill.

"I'm not what you think," he called, but she was fading into the remaining low-lying mist.

"Thanks for the map," Nat shouted, but she could never have heard.

She had blushed and giggled. Perhaps she'd liked him a bit, now he thought of it. He guessed she had, until he'd bullied her. She'd recognised him then. But he hadn't wanted her to go. He'd wanted her to stay and chat and let him stroke Conker.

He looked down at his filthy hands, his torn jeans stained with blood, and his trainers sodden and clammy. He was exhausted.

But he had to go on. If he didn't get to the bottom of the business with the little girl in the shed, no Jenny would ever trust him or like him again.

And time was running out. Jenny would tell her father: of that he felt certain.

Chapter Seventeen

NAT TUCKED the rain cape under his arm and trudged on uphill.

Jenny hadn't recognised him until he'd begun to throw his weight around. Nat thought back over the last three days. Nobody had recognised him until he had started to behave strangely: like when he had asked the way to the non-existent station at the village shop, or unless he had come over tough.

When he was being ordinary nobody connected him with the boy in the newspaper.

He'd always been so sure everyone had it in for him. The best tactic he'd come up with was to hit back first, so that they got the message they couldn't get anything over him. He hadn't been able to hit back over the last few days. He'd had to keep a grip on himself ... and ... people had liked him, been friendly even.

Jenny had blushed and giggled. Stanley had given him breakfast and was happy to tell him all about the birds. The vicar had been keen to see him and had complimented him on his caterwauling. And that twit, Zero, he had thought Nat a hero! Right at the beginning, the old lady in the train had assumed he was some nice kid, someone's pet grandson.

Maybe ... maybe everyone out there could like him, if he didn't get tough and turn them off. Maybe they weren't all out to knock him down.

Nat stopped for a second and stared down the hill at the yellow ball of sun rising above the horizon, flooding the heathland with warm light.

"Me," he muttered, grinning to himself. "I'm all right then!"

There was nothing wrong with him. He could get it right.

He'd get it all sorted out, get home, look after Mum, catch up on his maths with Miss Barnes so that he could go on to the upper school with the other kids. That Mr Prendergast might help him sort it out, because, come to think of it, even he might have been friendly if Nat hadn't nosed in his drawer and snitched his Niblets.

He wasn't stupid: he could do OK at school, if he went regularly.

Afterwards he would get a decent job, with money to buy what they wanted to eat at the supermarket, and money to go out with Sean and Gemma and Adam at the weekend.

Nat could see how simple it was. Why hadn't he seen it before? He'd been so busy fighting ...

The sun shone, a touch of warmth in its rays now. The future looked good, and he felt happy. He couldn't wait to get this Professor Keeping thing sorted out and get back to Mum.

He checked the envelope – a bit soggy from his sweating, but still safe.

He ran on in his squelching trainers, scarcely noticing the aching in his legs now.

He'd come back to this place again, he really would. Bring Mum. She'd love it. He'd write to Jenny, return her map, and see if she'd like to show them round.

He'd reached the ridge. The view to either side was spectacular. Beneath him, to the left, he could see another wide valley. That must be where Little Ebbs-bourne was.

Sure enough, among trees at the far end of the valley, he could see an expanse of glistening red roof tiles and a forest of chimneys.

Saturday morning, early still, and he'd made it! The thrill of triumph beat anything he'd felt winning a fight.

The house was big. He could make out a long drive leading out of the trees, down to huge entrance gates opening on to a lane. Coghill Hall – that must be Coghill Hall, and Professor Keeping would be there!

Even as he watched, Nat saw two cars pausing outside the gates and turning into the drive. He could just make out a sign attached to their roofs. Taxis. People were arriving at the conference already.

Behind the two cars came a white van which drove

past the gate and braked sharply. Its two back doors were flung open. Nat watched with interest as dark figure after dark figure, jumped down from the back.

Nat squatted down as the figures, ignoring the gates and drive, spread out at the foot of the hill. They looked like busy little black ants, scurrying forward, crouching down and then running on again.

Nat's elation evaporated. He froze despite the bright sun. He'd lost sight of the ants now, hidden in the bushes scattered at the bottom of the hill.

Who were they?

Nat leapt up as if a rocket had ignited inside him and dived into the wood ahead. He was so close now he wouldn't let anyone cheat him, stop him getting to Professor Keeping. They might be the police. Jenny could have already told her father.

Nat glanced at his watch. He'd wasted a good half-hour dawdling, daydreaming, enjoying the view. She could have got back. Her father would have phoned the police immediately.

Nat didn't mind the police; they wouldn't hurt him. He would just have to keep out of their way until they'd moved on, and then leg it down to Coghill Hall.

But were they the police? They were all in dark clothes, but he hadn't been able to recognise a uniform.

What if they were sent by the men in the church? He had evaded them so far, but they would probably have found his kit bag and searched it by now. They'd know he still had the envelope with him.

He watched the ants: there were so many of them.

He'd never manage to escape them all. But if they caught him it was over. Think! Think clearly, calmly.

He had to get rid of the envelope, hide it. He'd try and make it to Professor Keeping. If they caught him without the envelope they might let him go. He'd tell Professor Keeping where he'd hidden it. That was it – drop it, hide it.

Nat stared frantically around. There was a heap of brown spiky leaves. Tightly curled green fronds were breaking through the dead mound. Nat kicked the mound with his feet. It was hollow beneath and dry. He quickly pulled out the envelope, wrapped it in the red plastic cape and stuffed the bundle beneath the dead leaves and pulled more back on top.

There were similar brown mounds all around. He'd have to remember it. A few feet away a small tree trunk slanted to one side with a newer trunk coming out from the base, at an angle. The two trunks made a rough V shape; V for Victory.

A shout from behind floated up the hill.

"Left of ridge. Thirty degrees south-south-west. No sighting yet. Over."

Nat glanced back at the mound and ran, crouching low.

"Charlie Three calling. No sighting, but the blighter can't have got far. Surrounding wood. Over."

"Charlie Five calling. Received instructions. Moving in. Over."

The voices were coming from all sides of the hill now, echoing in the still air. He had to keep calm, think, stay ahead. The fear had given way to a strange, grim exhilaration.

This was the final count he had dreaded so long, when everyone would be after him, against him.

But he'd bounce back, survive the count, he was sure of that now.

Jenny had liked him, Stanley had liked him. He was doing all right now, there was nothing wrong with him. He just had to keep going, get to Coghill Hall to prove it to everyone.

He moved like an animal, propelled by some basic survival instinct. Now he knew what a fox felt in front of the hounds. Everything seemed clearer, more intense. He heard the faintest voice from a walkie-talkie, every branch and twig that cracked. He wove in and out of sharp gorse bushes, prickly holly. Crouched under sodden dead bracken fronds.

He was zig-zagging round the ridge. He could see a man in black crawling uphill. There was another one to the left. They were above him. But he'd broken through the circle!

He wanted to run for it, but he must control himself, be cunning, continue zig-zagging down, past the van.

He sat back on his heels and broke off big brown leaves dried stiff on long brown stalks. He stuck several fronds in the front and back of the neck of his T-shirt, and in the back of his jeans. In cautious quick runs, from prickly bushes to sheltering copse, he made his way down.

His back was soaked with dew – or was it sweat?

Drops trickled down his face, stinging his eyes, salty in his mouth.

The man sitting in the front of the van stared ahead with glazed eyes, more intent on listening to his headphones than on looking around.

"... he's got to be up there, Charlie Six. I mean, dammit, we've got eighteen boys on the job. Over."

Nat could hear crackling but couldn't hear the reply.

"Calling Charlie Six," the man persisted. "What's wrong with your receiver? Like I said, he's only a kid. Don't tell me none of you have got him in your sights. We've got to have him, or it will be murder from the boss. Over."

Nat crept past, ducking beneath the windows, making for the drive.

Then he heard the distant drone. He knew that drone. He'd heard it before, beside the railway track. He looked up at the clear blue of the sky. There it was, a black smudge, coming closer.

Whoever was in that microlite would spot him in an instant when it was overhead. He'd be trapped, unable to move, ripe for the little black ants.

His breath came in sharp bursts now, as if a rope was being pulled tighter and tighter round his chest.

Run for it.

Nat backed away from the drive – too exposed. Instead he edged round the base of the hill. Beneath the brow of the hill, but to one side of the drive was a low farmhouse. Holiday home, Jenny had said.

Nat plunged into the hedge, shoving his shoulders

through, scarcely noticing the cutting, scratching branches.

He emerged on a lawn dotted with neat flowerbeds. The droning was closer now, almost overhead.

At the edge of the lawn a terrace ran along the redbrick wall of an old house with a thatched roof. The glass doors on to the terrace were wide open, and a man with tousled brown and white grizzled hair, wearing a red dressing gown and slippers, sat in a wicker chair reading a newspaper. Nat could smell coffee from the pot and cup on the wicker table beside him. There was toast in a china rack, a dish of butter, a jar of jam.

Nat stood there, paralysed with surprise at the homely scene. The man looked up through gold-rimmed spectacles, as if suddenly sensing Nat was there.

"Beautiful morning, isn't it?" the man smiled with a flash of gold tooth. "Gorgeous sun after all that miserable rain. Spring at last!"

"I'm ... I'm ..." Nat's voice trembled, despite himself.

He was aware now of how he looked, leaves stuck all over him, covered in mud and scratches and dew.

"Bit of a mess, aren't you," said the man with concern. "Not to worry, young man. Come and find a pew, and I'll see about some plasters for those grazes. Coffee and toast? How nice to have company for breakfast."

"Coffee?" Nat stared blankly.

156

"Tea! Of course, boys tend to prefer tea, with sugar, but some fresh, warm toast – how about that? Go on, boy, go in, make yourself at home. It's so seldom I get a visitor. I'll get Mrs Thorn to make the tea and toast."

Nat tore away the dried leaves from his T-shirt, walked in a daze through the open glass doors, and sank on to the nearest seat.

The sofa was soft, and covered in green velvet. His dirty, scratched hands stroked the silky fabric. The room was quiet and peaceful. Rays of sunlight picked out heavy dark beams on the low ceiling and made the brass coalscuttle in the enormous fireplace sparkle.

People were mostly kind, he knew that now; and to think he had never even noticed before. He'd stay a bit, wait until the ants had gone, slip back up the hill and retrieve the envelope.

Deep in the house he heard the chime of a clock. Through the windows came the whirring of the micro-lite.

How distant the microlite seemed from the clock chiming in the house and the creaking springs of the velvet sofa. Nat was cradled in softness, dreaming of hot toast and strawberry jam.

After a few minutes, a thin lady wearing a clean flowery apron slipped in to the room, drew up a table in front of Nat, and set down a tray. Nat was glad she didn't try and chat and question him.

He attacked the hot toast without waiting for the man. He could have eaten enough for three! He sipped down the sweet tea. When he'd finished he felt sleepily lazy, but so much better.

The door opened and the man in the dressing gown and slippers came back and stood by the sofa.

"Looks as if you needed that!" he laughed, taking off his spectacles and laying them on a side table.

"Oh," Nat exclaimed. "I was so hungry ... It looked so good, I couldn't wait."

"Of course," smiled the man, as if this was how he expected all boys to behave. "Best meal of the day, breakfast, I always think. Have some more." He smiled broadly, holding out the rack of toast. "Be my guest, I insist ... You see, I've been waiting for you."

Nat's hand halted in its reach for a piece of toast.

The door opened and a man in a dark suit walked over to the glass terrace doors. He shut and locked them. Then the man in the dressing gown picked up a hand bell from a side table. It pealed with a high, tinkling ring.

The door opened again, and another man in a dark suit and tie walked swiftly over until he stood in front of Nat. Nat hardly dared look up at the harsh eyes above him, one dark and unfathomable, the other half-hooded in a drooping wink.

"The papers, Nathan," said the man in the dressing gown quietly, "and we need take it no further."

"I ... " Nat choked. "I don't have them. And it's too late. The police ... the girl's father will have called them. They'll be here soon, looking for me."

"Very true." The man rubbed his spectacles

158

thoughtfully on his sleeve. "They were tipped off as to your whereabouts. Your face is everywhere – television news, newspapers. We knew we only had to bide our time for you to be spotted, and the hounds set after you."

"The hounds?" Nat stuttered. "... The police on the hill?"

"The hounds drove you to us, straight into our arms. Now – you will tell us where the papers are or we shall force you to tell."

"You can't hurt me!" Nat shouted.

He knew that for sure: no one could hurt him. He was tough. He had bothered other children in the past, and sometimes he had had to take it back, usually at the hands of older boys. Bullying was a language he understood.

The man in the dressing gown settled back in the chair opposite and surveyed Nat. Then he turned to the man with the drooping eyelid.

"Bring me the phone." He swivelled round to face Nat. "Your mother: what time does she get back from work, Nathan?" His eyes never left Nat's face. There was a flash of gold as he smiled. "Have her watched," he continued to the man beside him. "Get Carl on to her."

"Mum! You leave her alone!" Nat tried to struggle to his feet, but he was pushed sharply down. "She'll be out of her mind already with worry. If you go near her I'll – I'll ..." His mother would crumble, collapse in an instant, like the little girl in the shed. "I don't care what you do with me, but if you touch her ..." Nat's fists were so tense they could have smashed the table apart.

"It is in your hands, dear boy," said the man softly. "Quite simple really: you will direct us to the envelope, or we shall have to visit your mother."

Nat took in a slow, deep breath. "In the church. In the room at the back – in my kit bag, stuffed under the bench," he gabbled.

He'd get rid of them. Then he'd be off, before they discovered his lie and had time to get back to him. They wouldn't get Mum: he'd give himself up to all those police and tell them what the men were after.

"Let me go now!"

He was close to tears. A cold, icy anger was eating away at him, but he daren't show it.

No one had pinioned him down like that before – knocked him down. He was beaten. Wouldn't survive the count. He wanted to wail and cry and kick out. No! He wouldn't give them the satisfaction.

"I can go now," he said, trying to sound polite, accommodating, but his guts churned with loathing of the man in his expensive dressing gown.

"Dear me, no! We shall not let you go until we have Dr Buxton's paper, and then we must insist you remain our guest until we are out of the country. Mrs Thorn!"

Nat could have banged his head against a wall.

How could he be so dumb! Of course they wouldn't let him go. He knew too much now. They wouldn't ever let him go. They had tried to get rid of the little girl, and they wouldn't hesitate to get rid of him.

He'd have to tell them about the envelope when they got back. They'd be mad with him. He had at most an hour to think; they'd surely need an hour to get to the church and back.

Nothing was worth hurting his mother for. She'd had a hard time since his father had left her, and she wasn't a good manager at the best of times. Nat hadn't helped either, but he loved her. She was all he had and she loved him.

The door opened, and the thin lady in the flowery apron came in. She ignored Nat and stood expressionless beside the man in the dressing gown.

"Yes, sir, you called?"

"I did, Mrs Thorn. Be so good as to open the door to the cellar and bring me the key."

"Yes, sir."

Fingers tightened round Nat's shoulders, digging into his armpits, pulling him up. Nat dragged his feet, until the man with the drooping lid gave his shin a vicious kick. Nat yelped. Half-dragging, half-carrying him, they bundled Nat down a passage to a door – that gaped into a well of darkness.

The hands shoved Nat forward. He stumbled down steps into the dark, while behind and above him a key turned in the lock.

His breath came in sharp pants, and something thundered and pounded in his ear.

It's all right ... Only darkness.

161

Nat drew in a deep breath and let it out with a slow hiss. The pounding in his ears slowed too.

He was mixed up in something pretty big. No one would risk treating kids like this if there wasn't something big at stake. The story he could tell the police now: abducting a boy, locking him away. They would be in real trouble when they were caught – if they were caught.

Nat swiped at the tears on his face, tears of hurt and of rage. It had all been going so well – at last. He had really thought he could win.

But he never had won.

Nat sank against the steps, his head sagging in his hands. One ... two ... three ... He couldn't block out the count hammering away in his head.

Chapter Eighteen

N AT SAT there stunned, in a stupor of despair. He
lifted his head dully. He had to wake up, move.

He could see a little now – the paler outline of the
steps. The cellar wasn't as dark as it had first seemed. A
grey light was seeping in from somewhere.

He stood up and felt his way along damp walls
towards the light. The passage opened into a rough
room with a cracked stone floor. A square of light
streamed through a small high window, glassless but
criss-crossed with iron bars. The cellar room was filled
with old furniture: an iron bedstead, wicker garden
chairs, gardening tools and racks of dusty wine
bottles.

Nat pushed a wicker chair underneath the window
and he stood on it. His outstretched hands could just
reach the window bars. He heaved himself up and
glimpsed a garage with a car reversing out of it before
he fell back. Nat listened as the car braked, then
accelerated away.

They were going to the church, to look for the envelope. He had so little time.

He pulled himself up again on the bars. The thin lady in the flowery apron was walking past with a basket of washing.

"Hey, missus! Let me out of here. I can explain—"

But she had gone, hadn't even glanced in his direction.

Nat dropped to the floor and stared round the dusty grey cellar.

Why bother? The men would be back soon. He'd tell them where the envelope was because nothing was worth risking Mum being hurt. They'd take the envelope and be away, out of the country before the police found him. Surely the police would find him soon enough – they must be looking everywhere.

If the girl was still in a coma, or ... dead, he hadn't a chance. He'd be taken into court with a blanket over his head. He'd seen it on telly. And there would be lots of women outside screaming, "Murderer!" or "We'll get you!", banging on the police car. And Mr Prendergast would get his way; have him locked up in some prison school.

No one would believe him: why he'd run off, tried to sort it out himself.

He was so tired. This morning he had thought he could change things, but he couldn't beat the men in suits.

"Haven't a hope," he muttered to himself as he

kicked the wine rack full of clattering bottles. "Never could last the final round."

The grey light had moved round on the walls, lighting up new corners of Nat's prison.

He ran his hands idly through the gardening basket on the rickety table beside him. It was full of junk: a ball of rough string, a trowel and fork, a plastic container of little blue pellets, a small cardboard tube of powdery stuff. Nat held them up to the light and peered at the labels: Slug and Snail Pellets, Hormone Rooting Powder.

There was a little brown package, no thicker than his thumb, with some thread like a candle wick sticking out of the twisted paper at the top. Nat peered at the tiny print. SMOKEOUT! the label proclaimed. *Effectively smokes out wasp and bee colonies.*

Nat was about to peel off the paper to see what was inside, when he read: *Directions. Do* NOT *disturb the paper. Light wick with care, keep pets and children away. When wick begins to smoke, insert into nest or hole.*

Nat sat back, an idea taking shape in his mind.

A match. He needed a match.

He emptied the gardening basket on the floor. No matches! He searched the cellar, exploring round the wine racks, rummaging in the dust beneath the garden furniture. He must have a match ... Surely there was a match.

Grit lodged under his nails, and a nail split as it grated against an old cupboard. Nothing.

165

The lock on the door. Maybe he could smash the lock.

He grabbed a spade and edged into the dark area at the foot of the steps. He stumbled up the steps and hammered at the lock, the noise ringing out and echoing round the cellar. He couldn't budge it. The lock was new, of cold, unrusted steel.

The spade slid from his hands, through the slatted steps, and landed on the floor with a soft thud.

The spade! It hadn't clattered on the stone floor. It had thudded softly. Nat crawled round and into the space beneath the steps.

Gritty rocks. Coal. Too crumbly to break the lock. A stack of newspapers beside a little stack of wood, and ... His hands trembled as they closed round the tiny box perched on top. Gingerly, Nat's fingers explored the box. Something rattled ... little sticks scattered on the floor: matches!

Nat carried a handful back into the grey room. He couldn't believe it. It must be the fuel store for the big fireplace. Nat picked up the packet of SMOKEOUT.

Careful! There was only one packet. He couldn't make a mess of it. Where should he put it?

He could put it on the stairs, where the smoke would quickly rise, but it might go out there. What had he learnt in Cubs? A fire needs oxygen, a draught. He should keep it in line with the window.

Nat positioned the tiny parcel on an upside-down flower pot on top of the wicker table. Then he scraped a match across the stone floor. It lit, but it blew out.

The second match he cupped in his hand, gently blowing on it. He held it to the wick. Nothing happened. The match went out and the wick turned black. Nat was about to strike a third match when he noticed a tiny glow of red and a thin wisp of smoke.

Quickly he fanned the SMOKEOUT with his hands. Smoke started pouring out, streams of revolting-smelling smoke.

Nat coughed and buried his nose in his sleeve. It was working faster than he expected. His eyes were beginning to smart.

"Fire! Fire!" His screams seemed to come from another body.

He held his breath while he kicked over the gardening basket, hurtled a spade against the wall, toppled the iron bedstead, and sent a stack of pottery flower pots crashing to the floor.

"Help! Fire! Fire!"

The smoke was billowing up. It was difficult to breathe. He stumbled out of the grey room to the foot of the steps, pulling himself in tight against the wall.

How long would the smoke last? It was only a small package.

Suddenly he heard voices above him, and the rattle of the door.

"We're not to go in, Pete," shouted a woman's voice. "He told us we're strictly not to go in."

"I don't know about the boy," a gruff voice answered, "but it makes no sense to burn the house down. If the house burns down, Barbara, it won't only be me who'll be out of my job."

"We can't call the fire brigade. Oh, what will—?"

"Get me the key, woman, and shut your mouth."

"I can't. It's in his room on his bedside table, and I'm not allowed—"

"Come along!" shouted the man, his voice breaking in fury. "The cellar's burning, Barbara, and the boy's there. Once the fire gets to the thatch there won't be any bedrooms left to mind! And what about that lady they stuck in the attic?"

Feet clattered away and then pounded back.

"Pete, there's smoke coming out of the cellar window."

The key rattled in the lock. A light went on above the steps and the door burst open. A big man in brown overalls stamped down the steps carrying a bucket, followed by the woman in her flowery apron holding a washing-up bowl.

Nat crouched down. As soon as he heard them coughing in the grey room, he ran up the steps and headed along the passage to the kitchen. The back door was open, barred only by a large pair of muddy boots.

Nat's shoes crunched on the gravel as he tore past the garage, clambered over the wooden five-bar gate and landed in the lane.

They would have seen him or heard him running past the cellar window. It wasn't worth hiding now. He had to run, run for his life.

He was like a deer. His feet lifted and bounded as if

they were flying. Down the lane, in through the big wrought-iron gates of Coghill Hall, up the drive.

A hoot behind him. Only a taxi driving past with a curious face peering from the window. His lungs were bursting, but he would never stop, never tire now.

The drive ended in a circular area where cars were parked and turning. Who were all these people milling around, carrying briefcases, raincoats over dark-suited arms?

Nat darted in and out, through glances of disapproval, murmurings of disgust.

Someone was shouting.

He must get in before they stopped him; find a rock, a piece of wood, and break a side window; shout for Professor Keeping ... Find the Professor before the men in dark suits got to Nat first.

"Nathan! STOP! AT ONCE!"

They knew him. He'd been recognised already.

He tore across a flowerbed, trampling the flowers. Someone was pounding down the other side of the bed.

Turn. Go back.

But huge arms dragged him backwards, toppled him off his feet. Nat could see the shiny black shoes, the stripe of the dark suit. He kicked at a trousered leg, revealing a striped sock and ... a dark brown leg.

Nat twisted back, staring up into the grim brown eyes.

"I've got you now, Nathan," said Mr Prendergast. "You're not going anywhere now. You're staying right by me, you understand?"

Nat nodded. The grip around his waist was like a vice.

"If I let go, Nathan, you are to stand in front of me and not move. Do you agree?"

Nat nodded again.

He was dropped to the ground. Wearily he turned round to see Mr Prendergast loosen his tie, shake out a clean white handkerchief from his pocket and mop his brow.

"Oh my God, Nathan! I thought I'd never find you," he gasped. Then he bent forward to catch his breath. "I'm a welfare officer, Nathan, not a bloomin' athlete."

He stood up, and surveyed Nathan from his towering height. "I've seen prettier sights," he said at last. Then he laid an arm firmly round Nathan's shoulder. "And I should warn you, Nathan: I'm very angry – the dance you've led me! There's a lot we are going to have to talk about."

Chapter Nineteen

THEY WERE in a spacious dining room lined with ancient portraits on the walls. The empty table at which they were sitting was covered with a crisp white tablecloth. Mr Prendergast had managed to procure drinks and sandwiches from somewhere.

Nat pushed his plate away. The last thing he felt like was eating. Mr Prendergast hadn't touched his either. Come to think of it, Mr Prendergast looked a bit ill and yellow.

"You made enough fuss on that train, Nathan, drew attention to yourself. I gather they were forced to make an emergency stop. But when the police boarded it at the next station, it didn't take them long to work out it was you."

Nat pulled a stupid face. What was he supposed to say?

"It isn't something to be proud about," rumbled Mr Prendergast. "I gather you gave some elderly passengers quite a shock."

Nat struck a straw into an apple-juice carton on the tray in front of him. Anything to avoid the questions. It was too complicated to explain now. All that mattered was that he'd persuaded Mr Prendergast to agree to his surrender condition.

"And that man in the village shop in Little Whittington. Said you came in looking as if you'd been sleeping rough, panting because you'd missed the bus. He recognised you as soon as you asked for the station, and didn't pay."

"He didn't ask me. I forgot," said Nat angrily.

"Very helpful man he was. He said other people concerned about you had been making enquiries as to your whereabouts. He asked around the village for us, so that the police and I went straight to the farm."

Nat sat silent, aware of Mr Prendergast's eyes boring into him. Mr Prendergast hadn't believed him, but he would in a few minutes. Nat would be able to explain it all.

Nat stared at the looming shape across the table.

"That little lad at the farm had found your note to your mother," Mr Prendergast stopped, his voice softer, his eyes never leaving Nat's face. "He was in tears. Quite taken to you he had. Said you were the best spy ever and he wouldn't believe you were wicked!"

"I helped him with his lamb," Nat muttered, remembering the wriggling rough wool beneath his hand.

"What's that got to do with it?" said Mr Prendergast with exasperation. "He said you were going to

172

Salisbury. Every time we came up with Salisbury, always Salisbury. Why?"

Nat didn't need to answer. It was as if Mr Prendergast was talking it through, trying to make sense of it himself.

"Then the trail went cold until we heard from this elderly vicar. The vicar said he didn't believe it of you for a minute. Didn't watch television or listen to idle gossip himself, but that a girl in his choir thought you were the boy on television."

Nat nodded. It sounded right. It had to be straggly Linda or Emma, the pink strawberry whip.

"Then this man in hospital seems to have picked up a hitch-hiker, a boy like you, who crashed his car. A touch of concussion there because, Nat, I don't think even you could drive a car."

It was good sitting with Mr Prendergast. The sheer size of the man was comforting, even if he was in an unaccustomed striped suit. And the men in dark suits … Surely they wouldn't dare touch him if he was with Mr Prendergast?

"Next we knew, a man called Stanley phones the police this morning – says he was birdwatching with you! You know what it's like, Nat. The police get weird calls from all over the place in cases like this. We didn't follow that up, of course, and then the police got this call from the father of a girl—"

"Jenny Livingstone of Boveridge Farm," put in Nat. He mustn't forget her name. He would send her map back.

"My God, Nathan. How can you just sit there and talk so coolly! I thought you'd gone mad or something, and here you are calmly giving me details ..."

"Go on," said Nat.

"Anyway she said you were going to Little Ebbs-bourne. The police had a squad of searchers up on that hill as fast as you can say Nathan Price, and I tore down here in my car to find Little Ebbsbourne was just a cluster of farms around Coghill Hall. I couldn't work out why on earth you were so anxious to get here."

"And I broke through the police circle," said Nat.

"So you did," said Mr Prendergast grimly.

"But how did you spot me?"

"When the police couldn't find you, I came up to Coghill Hall to see if I could use the fax machine and report back to my department. I wanted to call your mother too, to ask her if she knew why you had headed here. And, blow me, if I don't find you leaping around, trampling the rose bushes, looking like a tramp and vagrant. So tell me, Nathan, what *are* you up to? I need to know, and quickly, because you're in very big trouble."

"You'll see," said Nat triumphantly. "When Professor Keeping comes, I'll explain everything then."

"And the girl?" said Mr Prendergast suspiciously.

"Especially the girl."

"You'd better, Nathan!" exploded Mr Prendergast. "Professor Keeping is a very important man, head of the medical conference here. I felt bad asking, insisting he talk to us. He only agreed when he heard the police were involved. Asking a man like that to come and talk to a runaway boy and his social worker, in the middle of a major conference—"

The door to the dining room had swung open.

At a brisk pace a small dapper man in blue – blue suit, pale blue shirt and striped navy tie – came over to them. The expression of irritation was obvious on his face and he examined, with deliberation, the watch on his wrist. A white badge with bold black letters was attached to his lapel: PROFESSOR KEEPING.

"Mr Prendergast, this is the boy I presume," the Professor had a quick, precise way of speaking. "I have a bare five minutes I can give you."

Nat gulped. Where should he begin?

This was what he had come for, struggled through everything for, and the man could only spare five minutes. He hadn't pictured the meeting like this.

"Dr Buxton – It's about Dr Buxton. She's not here."

"We know, we know," said the Professor rapidly. "She won't be here to read her paper. Severe influenza, I understand."

Nat struggled to find the words, staring in panic at Mr Prendergast.

"It's her little girl," Mr Prendergast helped. "Nathan believes he has something to tell you about her girl ..."

Professor Keeping tapped the table top with his fingers. "We have sent Dr Buxton our best wishes. A great disappointment for her, not to be able to read her paper. We are all expecting great things of it. In fact I

175

would say the conference has really been organised as a means of disseminating her breakthrough."

"Disseminating?" said Nat. What was the Professor going on about?

"Yes." The Professor pursed his lips, arching his fingers so that both hands touched at the fingertips. "Dr Buxton believes she has engineered a drug that will prevent the collapse of the immune system, as in the case of illnesses such as AIDS and certain cancers. Quite revolutionary! This conference is to enable her to convey her results and methods publicly. In fact" – the Professor pushed his sleeve up over his watch – "we are to hear the paper in twenty-two minutes' time."

Nat sat up. Now he would explain!

"You can't," he said fiercely. "She's not here. She's been kidnapped."

The Professor looked at Mr Prendergast and shrugged his shoulders. Nat could guess what he was thinking – that Nat was a 'problem', 'disturbed' even, and that Nat was Mr Prendergast's responsibility.

"So, Mr Prendergast, if the boy has only some tall story to tell me, I must go and welcome Dr Buxton's assistant, check that all the delegates have a photocopy of Dr Buxton's paper – much still to do."

"Copy of Dr Buxton's paper?" gasped Nat. "You can't have Dr Buxton's paper. I've got her paper – on the hill – under the dead leaves, next to the tree ..."

The Professor was no longer listening. He turned to Mr Prendergast, as if Nat was now invisible.

"Dr Buxton's apologies arrived this morning. Of

course we are disappointed, but we understand the situation. And she has sent her assistant, Dr Ridelsky, to read her paper in her stead."

"But—"

Nat was in a daze. He looked a complete fool! The envelope didn't matter; it could rot in the rain.

So there'd been another copy all along. That little girl could have misunderstood the whole situation and run away from nothing.

But – it didn't add up.

Nat went over it feverishly in his mind. Someone had hurt her, been after her.

"Someone else wants Dr Buxton's paper," said Nat desperately. "Someone else is after her."

The Professor looked pityingly down at Nat. "Of course there are always wild rumours, of some criminal gang interested in making money from medicine. In this case, if anyone could have got hold of Dr Buxton's research, altered a few insignificant details and registered the research as their own, they would have been sitting on a medical fortune. Their company could have been granted an exclusive legal licence to manufacture the drug for a number of years. No chance of that now," Professor Keeping's mouth stretched in a fleeting smile. "Dr Buxton is deliberately not claiming exclusive ownership, by making her work available to everyone through our international conference. Both poor and rich countries will have access to her research and be able to manufacture the drug for the benefit of their sick."

Nat was on his feet.

"That's it!" The words were jumping out of his throat now. "That explains it! The men in suits were after me because I had the paper about Dr Buxton's research, and I knew they had tried to get it off the little girl, and now—"

"And now," said Professor Keeping sharply, "I must leave you." He turned, but paused as if on an afterthought. "Mr Prendergast, if the boy is so interested, you can both sit at the back of the auditorium and listen. Mind you – only if I have your assurance the boy is under your complete control."

Nat peered down. They were sitting at the top of a semicircular auditorium with a clear view of the platform beneath them. Running in front of each row of plush seats was a table ledge equipped with a fresh pad of paper, pens, and a typed copy of Dr Buxton's paper.

Professor Keeping was leading a man on to the platform.

"So sad ... but so pleased ... Dr Ridelsky."

Professor Keeping sat down amid polite clapping. A man with thick, wavy brown hair was at the podium. He coughed into the microphone and started reading.

Nat didn't understand a word.

On and on droned the voice. The hands of the clock on the wall crept painfully round, five ... fifteen ... thirty-five ... fifty minutes. Even Mr Prendergast was yawning.

Nat watched the wavy brown head bent over the podium droning on. The auditorium was full of men and women listening intently, poring over the paper in front of them, scribbling notes here, adjusting headphones there. Then Nat saw that even one or two of these had started yawning, or staring into space.

"Satisfied?" said Mr Prendergast with obvious relief as thin clapping broke out again.

Nat followed Mr Prendergast and joined the queue for the exit.

He felt crushed, squeezed dry like the crumbling sponge in the bathroom at home. He didn't know what was going on any more.

Had he got it all wrong? Could the little girl have fallen and banged her head, poking round the shed.

He'd been so convinced that all would be revealed, explained, if only he found Professor Keeping. Now his last bit of hope had gone.

Knocked down.

"All the way have I come – for this," a lady in a black suit and big gold earrings was saying in a strong foreign accent. "What is it, I ask you? What is new? Have I not heard of all this before?"

"Yes, after all the hype, I must agree," replied a man carrying a pile of papers. "I rearranged all my teaching load at university to get to this congress. Very naughty of Professor Keeping to entice us all with stories of a major breakthrough."

Nat stared at Dr Buxton's paper in his hand. He hadn't even bothered to look at it.

He flipped the pages. They were more closely typed than he remembered, and that diagram, on page two, with lots of figures underneath: it wasn't there. The paper didn't have the diagram anywhere. He turned to the last page. Twelve pages. There had been fifteen pages, he was sure of it ...

"Mr Prendergast!" Nat tugged on the big arm. "This isn't Dr Buxton's paper. I know it isn't ..."

"Dr Ridelsky – do come this way. I'm so sorry you won't be staying. But I must say how grateful ..."

Professor Keeping was walking up the steps beside the man with the thick brown hair. The Professor's step had lost its brisk bounciness and his voice was flat.

"Do have a drink before you leave," the Professor pushed Nat back with his arm as they brushed by.

The man beside him glanced over Professor Keeping's outstretched arm. Nat was sure Dr Ridelsky had spotted him: a fleeting smile hovered beneath a drooping lid before he turned away.

A chill like an icy finger ran up Nat's spine.

He grabbed Mr Prendergast's arm. "Did you see him? The droopy wink? And that hair: it's a wig. I'm sure it's a wig."

"Nathan!" Mr Prendergast said sharply. "That – is – enough! I've got the police waiting for you outside. You've had your chance. Now we've got to deal with them."

Mr Prendergast stood back to let a lady past. He was too big to share the narrow passage.

Nat ducked and crawled on his hands and knees

behind a row of seats and pushed into the queue making for the exit on the other side. His face was flushed and burning, but he was through the door before Mr Prendergast had turned round.

No, he wasn't ready for the police – yet. The police and Mr Prendergast would have to wait, stop the count.

Chapter Twenty

NAT'S THROAT was tight and his chest felt as if it was gripped by an iron band. His fists were clenched, ready to hit out, punch hard. He wasn't believed!

He had never for a moment thought it would come to this. To fight so far and be disqualified before the deciding round ...

He kept his head down and tried to hide among the chatting delegates as they pushed their way out.

"I was going to stay the full two days Professor de Crespigny," said a tall willowy man beside Nat, "but I'm not sure the congress is of sufficient interest. I've got a pile of term papers to mark at college, and we've discussed this material before."

"*Absolument*, Dr Barrington!" replied a man with a neat white beard turning in front of Nat. "Of course zis will do much damage to Dr Buxton's reputation – zat tired paper. We 'ave all 'eard of her brilliance, but where was it? I saw no brilliance."

"Excuse me," Nat said, pushing his way through.

He had to get past the throng before they stopped their complaining and noticed him.

Ahead of him a young man in a black waistcoat and bow tie carried a tray of clinking bottles. If he could get in behind that waiter ...

Nat snatched an empty mineral-water bottle from a table in the passage and followed close on the waiter's heels.

The waiter hurried on down the passage, through some swing doors, and disappeared. Nat waited a few seconds and then followed, holding the bottle out in front of him.

He was at the top of the back staircase. Nat crept down until he was level with a door through which he could hear a radio playing, the clatter of plates, and voices singing. Judging by the cooking smells it was the kitchen.

The door was kicked open. A woman's leg, in black stockings and black skirt, held the door back.

"Don't forget table nine ... That Dr Rossetti is for the vegetarian lasagne," a man's voice called from the kitchen, "and Professor Finkelstein, on table eleven, is having the kosher meal."

"OK, Sam," called the black leg and skirt, yelling back over her shoulder. "These table numbers get me all in a muddle ..."

Nat slipped rapidly along the passage and pushed open the door beyond. The smell was awful. He was surrounded by huge garbage bins, empty packing cases for bottles and bundles of newspapers tied up with string.

Nat crouched behind a bin. He had to think.

He had to get the envelope. Barely an hour ago he'd hoped he was finished with it. If only he'd known, instead of sitting through the lecture, he could have gone back for it.

There was precious little time now. He couldn't evade Mr Prendergast and the police for long.

That 'assistant', Dr Ridelsky, would be gone. Nat had to show them that the man was a fraud, that he was the same man who had thrown Nat down the cellar steps only hours before; that the paper the man had read was not the same as the one Nat had found in the shed.

At last he'd pieced it all together, understood it all, but he couldn't convince anyone of the truth!

It didn't surprise him. With his record he should have known no one would listen to him. A loser, handicapped on points before he had even set foot in the ring.

He pulled himself stiffly up and edged round the bin. He was tired, very tired. His legs were as cold and heavy as stone.

The garden with its neat rosebeds spread out around him. He'd better not go down the drive – he'd soon be spotted there. In the distance he could see the hill. The only way was to cross the garden, climb the gate into the field, go over the field and up the hill, avoiding the lane.

Nat was already across the lawn, heading straight for the gate in the hedge, when he heard men's voices coming towards him. There were two men, folders and papers in their hands, deep in conversation. He couldn't be noticed. He'd wait for them to pass.

"... Dr Buxton has got nowhere. Now Professor Sind, at Jaipur University, is making remarkable progress with his antagonistic molecular hypothesis. That's where the future in research ..."

Nat grabbed a garden fork standing up in the rosebed beside him and started poking at the soil.

"I wasn't sure of Professor Sind's paper in the *Journal of Immune Deficiency*, last September, was it? Now, what roses are these?"

Nat's heart thumped so violently he was sure they could hear it. He kept his back to the voices behind him and went on prodding the soil.

"Do you know what roses these are?"

A hand fell on his shoulder.

"Ugh," Nat grunted.

"My guess is they're hybrid musks, Felicia or Penelope."

"Ugh ... Musks."

"I thought so," the voice sounded pleased with itself. "Excellent the way they train these backward youngsters in horticulture" – the voice faded away – "find a useful role in society ..."

He mustn't hang around.

Nat walked fast across the lawn, forcing himself not to run. The gate was padlocked so he dragged his heavy legs up and over the bars. The field was ploughed and tiny green shoots were beginning to appear through the wet furrows. Nat's trainers got heavier and heavier. It was an effort to lift his mud-caked feet.

The only noise was of his heavy panting. No shouting. He hadn't been seen.

Through the gate at the far side. The white van was still there. Around it were the ants. Men in black sweaters and dark trousers, laughing and shouting. They were loading stuff into the back of the van and some had already climbed in on to the bench seats.

They'd seen him. But he had to go past them to get out of the field. He looked for a branch to scrape the chunks of mud off his shoes. The fork hanging heavy in his hand ... He'd brought it with him. He'd never noticed.

He put his head down and scraped his shoes with the prongs. Get them clean. They might be suspicious if they thought he'd come over the field. He knew they'd get him now, but he had to try. One last attempt, he thought wearily. Go down fighting.

"... feel cheated, I do. We did it all by the book and the bastard made it through."

"... and he just gives himself up, can you believe it, straight into the arms of his social worker."

"Never been a murderer round here before. Thirty years I've been in the service – hoped I'd go out with my picture in the paper."

"You will, Bill, when you get your retirement clock."

"Don't you be cheeky, young Potts. When you're my age you'll be lucky to get an eggtimer."

Nat walked steadily through the middle of them, his fork over his shoulder. If he looked shifty they'd be suspicious so he might as well tackle them head on. "Excuse me."

"You can go up now, lad. They've caught the bastard, up at the hall. Should be safe enough now. I remember when I used to come up rabbiting as a boy ..."

"When was that – dark ages, Bill?"

"Now look here," growled the older man. "If I wasn't in the force I'd give you a belting."

"I'd better watch out then, when you retire."

The chuckles grew fainter behind him.

Nat couldn't believe it – he was through!

He dropped the fork, bent over and scrambled up the hill. Where had he left the envelope? Beneath the top ridge, somewhere to the left.

Nat was approaching from a different direction. It all looked different. There were lots of brown leaf heaps with fronds poking through. Which one? There were so many. Frantically he ran from heap to heap, kicking them open with his feet. There was no sign of the envelope.

Voices had broken into excited shouting below.

Nat ran, half crazed, from dried heap to heap.

A distant thudding was coming closer.

The tree, that was it, the V shape. He ran from clump to clump, watching for the tree. The thudding

187

was heavier, and the shouting louder.

He fell over the next clump, put out both hands to rough trunks to haul himself free. Two trunks. Two arms. He was clinging to a V.

He plunged both his arms into the dried clump, wildly tearing at the dead fronds and pushing aside the fresh green bracken.

Wet and slimy, the cape was there. The thudding bore down on him and stopped abruptly.

"If – you – so much – as . . ." the deep voice gasped above him. Nat rolled over, pulled out the battered envelope and held it up to the furious brown eyes and face glistening with beads of sweat.

"The envelope," Nat whispered. "It's Dr Buxton's paper. It's here, under the leaves."

The purple flush seeped from Mr Prendergast's face. The fury gave way to a look of surprise, then bewilderment. Slowly he stretched out his hand and pulled Nat to his feet.

The excited face of the older policeman appeared over the brow of the hill, followed by the eager faces of the ants.

"Good God! We saw him – rabbiting. Handcuffs, I've got handcuffs," he shouted.

"We won't need them, officer," said Mr Prendergast. "I'm taking him back to Coghill Hall."

"Are you certain? Must be as slippery as an eel, that one. Are you sure he'll go quietly?"

The policemen stared at Nat with faces of horror and amazement.

"To Professor Keeping?" Nat asked.

"To Professor Keeping," panted Mr Prendergast. "I guess you know all about this, Nathan. I can't make head or tail of it, so you're going to have to explain it. But one thing you're not doing, is leading me on a run like this again! Another move and I'll agree to hand-cuffs."

Nat punched the air. His tiredness had vanished. He wanted to leap and shout and yell ... He could prove it, prove it all!

The hall was teeming with people standing in groups, chatting. Nat dodged in and out until he glimpsed Professor Keeping walking despondently in through the front door to the hall.

Nat pushed his way up to him and grabbed his arm.

"Professor Keeping, I've got it!" he shouted, waving the battered envelope in front of the Professor's tight face, "I've got Dr Buxton's paper!"

Faces turned at the commotion.

Professor Keeping's mouth set in a hard line as he drew his shoulders back.

"Take your hand off me! You should not be on the premises. Where are the police?"

Professor Keeping turned as if to summon help.

Nat tore open the envelope and shook the pages in front of the Professor's face.

"Look! You have to look! Look at the diagram on page two, and – and there are fifteen pages."

The Professor glanced down with distaste, and then

189

stared. For a moment he stood very still, then slowly he stretched out his hand and took the pages. Without a word he turned each page, went back to the beginning and examined the pages again.

He was like a man in a dream, oblivious to Nat standing in front of him. Then he coughed, looked round and cleared his throat: "Ladies and Gentlemen ..." His voice rose louder, and he smiled. "Ladies and gentlemen. May I have your attention! I believe I have a most remarkable announcement to make ..."

Chapter Twenty-one

THE YELLOW Volkswagen chugged out of Salisbury, with a police car following behind.

"Are you taking me home?" Nat asked.

"Not yet, Nathan. We've called your mother and she knows you're safe, but the police want to check everything out before releasing you."

"Don't they believe me?" said Nat, his frustration mounting. "Where are you taking me?"

"To St Mary's Hospital, in Rombridge." Mr Prendergast ground the gear stick down. "To visit that little girl."

So she was alive. Nat hardly dared ask.

"Is she all right – conscious?"

"Came round this morning. The police want to see if she recognises you, and that she backs up your story. Of course she might well have some memory loss, but she sounds lively enough – complaining to the nurses about the orange juice, going on about some revolting brew. It might be concussion still."

"I know what she wants," grinned Nat.

"I don't know, Nathan," said Mr Prendergast. "Why is it I'm always in the dark. You know everything and I appear to know nothing."

Nat laughed.

"And I hope you know what Dr Buxton's paper was about, because I didn't understand a word of it. Mind you – you saved the bacon of that Professor – the excitement at the end, like a flock of starlings twittering away."

"I saw a goshawk yesterday."

Mr Prendergast looked sideways at Nat, "Goshawk – is that a bird? You never told me you were interested in birds, just TV and boxing."

"I might be," said Nat indignantly. "I don't know till I find out, do I?"

Nat stared out of the window at the dusk descending over the misty hedgerows. They had stopped talking, but it wasn't an awkward silence.

"I wouldn't mind living in the country," he said at last.

"I spent three years in the country when I was around your age, in Jamaica."

"With your mum?"

"No." With one hand Mr Prendergast fished a yellow cloth out from under his seat and leant forward to clean the windscreen. "I was sent back to my grandfather – too much of a handful for my parents. They were both out at work all day, earning a living, so I did pretty much as I liked, which wasn't much."

"Did – did you bunk off school?" said Nat in astonishment.

"More than was good for me," Mr Prendergast chuckled. "But my grandfather soon put an end to that. He was a strict, but fair man. I wouldn't be in this job now if it wasn't for him." He tossed the duster into Nat's lap. "Give your side a clean. We'll be able to see where we're going then."

Nat stared out of the window as he rubbed. He was glad they were in the car – it was easier to talk when they didn't have to look at each other.

"I didn't like you when I first met you," said Nat. He remembered the open drawer and the shadow across the desk.

"And I didn't like you either, Nathan," laughed Mr Prendergast. "I saw a boy who wanted everything done for him, wanted it all on a plate, so he could choose whether he took it or kicked the plate away. Yep! I recognised a boy from way back in you."

Nat turned and examined the strong profile, barely visible in the fading light.

"I can go one better than that, Nathan," Mr Prendergast added. "I could have happily strangled you yesterday, when you looked on course to get me sacked from my first job."

Nat stared at the mass of dark suit and long legs, crammed into the little car.

Mr Prendergast certainly wasn't like Miss Milburn. He wouldn't be able to pull anything past Mr Prendergast when his back was turned.

It surprised him, but he didn't mind. In a strange way he felt safe. He knew where he was at last. He couldn't wait to get back, see Mum, boast to Gemma, Sean and Adam – even school and Miss Barnes.

"Did ... did you ever catch up on the stuff you missed at school?"

"Sure. It took some hard work – but a boy like you, with your determination, could do it too. All you need is an ogre behind you ..."

"You?" Nat grinned.

Mr Prendergast braked as they turned a corner. The car creaked and the tyres screeched in protest.

"I was in a chauffeur-driven limousine yesterday. It went so smooth you wouldn't believe you were moving, unless you looked out of the window."

"Oh yes, Nathan," said Mr Prendergast. "Tell me another! Bet it didn't have my grandad's *Jesus Saves!* sticker on the back window."

"No, it didn't. And my name's Nat."

The girl was sitting up in bed, propped against pillows, her fair curly hair shining and clean. On her bedside table PC Titchfield and the WPC had set up a tape recorder.

"You didn't leave me enough!" the little girl exclaimed as Nat and Mr Prendergast entered her room off the main ward. "It tasted lovely. Tell the nurses what it is, because they won't get it for me, and I'm so thirsty."

Nat could feel everyone's eyes on him. He was a fish in a bowl.

"I'll get you some," he muttered.

"Come here!"

Nat walked hesitantly up to her bed. Plump little hands tugged insistently on his arm, and then pulled his head to hers.

"I think I left Mummy's big envelope in your den," she whispered in his ear. "Ugh! You're dirty and smelly! I can't remember where I put it and I was meant to be looking after it – it was important and they can't find Mummy and I want her ..."

Suddenly the little girl shook with tears.

Nat's arms were yanked from behind, and he turned to look into the stern face of PC Titchfield.

"Come on, lad. We'll go on with this later. The doctor said not to upset her."

"Let go ..." Nat struggled, a memory flooding into his mind. He hadn't given a thought as to where they had taken Dr Buxton. "Dr Buxton, her mother ... I think ... I think she's in the thatched farmhouse close by the front gates of Coghill Hall. She'll be in the attic. I'm sure it's her!"

In his mind he could hear a man's voice shouting, on the other side of the cellar door: "... and what about that lady they stuck in the attic."

He'd been in such a panic to escape. He'd heard the shout, but it hadn't registered in his terrified mind.

The WPC pulled a phone from her belt, and walked rapidly to the door, talking urgently.

The little girl's face lit up with a wide smile. "I knew you'd help," she said to Nat.

195

"The envelope – it's all right," explained Nat gruffly. "I found it and took it to Professor Keeping."

"Thank you," she said politely. "I knew you were a kind boy."

The atmosphere in the room had changed. Nat turned, and everyone was smiling.

"Well, lad, I think we know enough now," the policeman said. "We got it wrong; but all the evidence was against you. Now we've got new information, and the girl – she knows you. I think it's going to be OK."

"What about those men? The man with the eye ..."

"We're trying to track them down. We'll need all the information you can give us, but so far they've got clean away." The policeman sighed. "They may be off our patch already. It's an international gang we're after. We've got a watch on all ports and airfields. So far as we've been able to piece it together, we know they want the results of Dr Buxton's research: this new miracle drug. They may have kidnapped Dr Buxton to try and persuade her to work for them, or they may be keen to keep her out of the way while they file the drug patent as their own invention. That way they'll make millions from exclusive sales of the drug. At all costs they wanted that research paper, and wanted to keep Dr Buxton from sharing it at that conference."

"But," said Nat, "why hurt ... ?"

"Because they guessed Sophie here had the paper. She had seen them too. She was too dangerous a witness to keep around. If you're right about her mother being in that attic, you'll have done most of our work for us," the policeman grinned. "Thought of a career in the police force?"

Nat was taken through it all. He had to fill in every detail of what had happened, until he stopped abruptly. A faint clattering echoed in the corridor outside. He knew that noise. It grew louder and louder until it was outside the door. The policeman looked at him in surprise.

"It's Mum!" exclaimed Nat. "Her steel tips ..."

The policeman looked annoyed.

"We told your mother we'd let her know the outcome and bring her to see you when we'd finished questioning you. But that's mothers, isn't it? Can't keep away. Think the sun rises and sets on their son's head."

Nat could hear Mum's breathless voice: "Is this Ward C? I know the police said they'd fetch me when they were finished with him, but I've been that worried – I couldn't wait. And I went to the wrong hospital. I wasn't sure which one she was in ... And then there were no buses. He is here, is he? He's a good boy. Tell me he's here."

The door burst open and Mum hesitated in confusion at the crowd around the bed.

"What's going on? Where's Nat? What's he done now?"

Mr Prendergast grabbed a white towel hanging at the end of Sophie's bed and chucked it over Nat's head. "He's here, Mrs Price, and we're about to present him with the Champion Boy's Belt. Flyweight, bantamweight – what is it, Nat?"

197

The towel shook.

"Heavyweight," came Nat's muffled voice and, grinning, he threw back the towel.

The policewoman had slipped back into the room, pushing Nat aside at the bed.

"Listen!"

She held her phone against Sophie's ear.

The little girl's eyes stared intently ahead.

"You're in a cottage ... with straw on the roof? I'm in a hospital ... You're coming to get me? Come quick and you can meet my new friend. No, a boy ... a big boy ... and he took your envelope to Professor Keeping and ... he made it all right."

Couldn't sound more simple, Nat thought, as he watched the smile spread across her face.

Also by
Elizabeth Hawkins

THE MAZE

Andrew didn't know Joanna any more. She wasn't the cheerful, noisy sister he was used to. Having to give up their home and move to stay with elderly cousin Beatrice, had upset her, made her mean and unfriendly. Maybe Andrew shouldn't worry. But maybe, just maybe, there is something terribly wrong . . .

"Elizabeth Hawkins has triumphed in creating a sensitive hero who has to fall back on his masculine virtues of creativity, protectiveness, courage and loyalty to save his sister from supernatural forces." *The Times*

ISBN 1 85213 854 8

SEA OF PERIL

A powerful novel based on a true second World War story.

Jimmy is aboard the *City of Karachi* bound for life in Canada. Although he feels homesick, he and his new friends treat the voyage as an adventure. But the adventure turns to tragedy when the ship is torpedoed and everyone is cast upon the treacherous Atlantic Ocean in small lifeboats. How will they survive in the storm-tossed sea?

ISBN 1 86039 065 X